BATTLETECH:

PAID IN BLOOD

THE HIGHLANDER COVENANT, BOOK TWO

BY MICHAEL J. CIARAVELLA

BATTLETECH: PAID IN BLOOD
By Michael J. Ciaravella
Cover art by Florian "SpOoKy777" Mellies
Cover design & layout by David Kerber

Printed in USA.

Published by Catalyst Game Labs,
an imprint of InMediaRes Productions, LLC
7108 S. Pheasant Ridge Drive • Spokane, WA 99224

CHAPTER 1

"I keep watching the news broadcasts, and all these talking heads keep harping on is the 'temporary lull in combat.' Does anyone know what the hell they are talking about?"

> —*San-ben-bing* Arvin Keno,
> Fourth McCarron's Armored Cavalry

FORWARD OPERATING BASE ROMEO
15 KILOMETERS EAST OF THE CITY OF TARA
NORTHWIND
REPUBLIC OF THE SPHERE
4 DECEMBER 3150

As she approached the camp's center, *Sang-shao* Lindsey Baxter, commanding officer of the Fourth McCarron's Armored Cavalry regiment, ran an appraising eye over the bustling encampment and nodded appreciatively at all the work Laurel's Legion had done in such a short time. Ever since the Legion had returned from the fighting on the continent of Kearney, they had been working day and night to prepare for impending battles with the defenders of Northwind: the Twelfth Hastati Sentinels and their recent Republic of the Sphere reinforcements from Terra.

Remembering the arrivals from the Republic capital, Lindsey's lips thinned in annoyance at the thought of how these reinforcements had jeopardized her mission. When she had first accepted the mission to capture the hyperpulse generator station on Northwind, her orders had come with the understanding that the beleaguered Republic, surrounded by enemies seeking to invade Terra, would have insufficient forces available to reinforce the planet once she began her assault. While she, of all people, knew how quickly things could change on the battlefield, she was very interested in meeting whomever had provided that intel analysis—preferably in a dark alley.

From the large tent ahead of her, the command center for the FOB, *Sang-shao* Julie Qiao, Baxter's counterpart from Laurel's Legion, stepped out, flanked by two of her officers. Like Lindsey, Qiao had bundled up against the brisk Northwind winter, but also seemed to be making a conscious effort not to let the cold affect her. Despite the lack of notice for Lindsey's visit, her fellow regimental commander nodded and flashed a smile tinged with true welcome.

"Good afternoon, *Sang-shao!*" Qiao said. "Welcome to Forward Operating Base Romeo."

Lindsey nodded. "I am sorry for dropping in on short notice, but I was eager to see how things were going out here, near the action."

Qiao smiled again at the insinuation, and Lindsey hoped her thoughts were not as apparent to the other *sang-shao's* officers. Her frustration at being far from the fighting was palpable, as she was not the sort of commander who did well with inaction. Her current duties, overseeing the continued protection of the Northwind HPG compound and the planet's capital city of Tara, had required her to stay close to the command center, which had left Qiao to oversee setting up of the forward staging area for future strikes at the Republic stronghold known as the Castle.

"How are things going back in the big city?" Qiao asked, dismissing her staff with a nod.

Despite the brisk winter chill, the two women walked slowly through the base, allowing Lindsey to get a good look at the preparations. All around them, technicians and MechWarriors were working to ready their equipment, taking the brief opportunity to rest and rearm before the conflict resumed in earnest. Laurel's Legion, one of the four Capellan Confederation allied military commands that had struck Northwind, had previously been posted to the smaller continent of Kearney, and while the Legion had not seen the heavy fighting Lindsey's regiment had during the first battle at the Castle, Qiao's troops had seen their own share of combat while fending off constant guerrilla strikes from Republic forces intent on reclaiming the Fort Barrett base on the Kearney coast.

"Slowly. The *gao-shiao-zhang* is on his way back to the city now." *Gao-shiao-zhang* Jiang Hui was the Grand Master of Warrior House Imarra, first among equals in the esteemed Capellan Warrior House Orders, and held senior command of the mission to claim Northwind. While Baxter herself was the senior-most commander from the regular Capellan Confederation Armed Forces, the unique relationship the Warrior Houses held with the rest of the CCAF made her defer to him in most matters, a state of affairs she was finding far too comfortable for her own liking. The pleasant, smiling warrior was not what she would have expected from the leader of all the vaunted Warrior Houses of the Confederation, but he had shown careful skill at deploying his forces, and had often solicited her advice, allowing her a significant amount of autonomy in her own actions on the mainland.

"And the Grand Master let you sneak out of the city while he was away?" Qiao asked suspiciously, glancing over with a knowing grin.

Lindsey kept her expression carefully composed, but allowed a playful lilt into her voice. "I thought it important to inspect our outlying areas while things were still quiet."

"Knowing there was no way he would let you do it once he returned," Qiao finished, and the two women shared a mutual smile. "Should I take that to mean we have heard nothing new from our recently arrived allies from the Draconis Combine?"

Any trace of humor quickly flitted from Lindsey's face, and she voice grew taut. "Oh, I have heard plenty from *Sho-sho* Ikeda's aide as they approached orbit, but nothing from Ikeda directly. He has made no move to land on Northwind, and is seemingly content to hold high orbit for now." She sighed heavily. "I just wish I knew what he was thinking."

Qiao remained silent, for which Lindsey was grateful. Despite their friendship, Lindsey doubted there was any possibility that her fellow *sang-shao* could have offered that would have made more sense than the ones she had endlessly considered.

Having captured both the HPG compound and the city of Tara, Lindsey had been in the process of seizing the Castle, the last redoubt for the Republic forces, when additional reinforcements from Terra had arrived, led by the legendary Countess Tara Campbell and her Highlanders. The Highlanders battalion, the newest incarnation of the historic Northwind Highlanders mercenary regiments, had returned to protect their homeworld, and had dropped nearly on top of Lindsey's own forces when they were only moments from victory. Unfortunately, the arrival of such significant Republic reinforcements had not only stymied her attempt to take the Castle, but had immediately put the Capellan troops on the defensive. With fresh Republic forces ready to roll over her damaged units, Lindsey had been forced to take a different path to reclaim the initiative, and had put out her own call for off-planet reinforcements.

To her chagrin, she had received them from an unexpected source.

Sho-sho Hisao Ikeda was the commander of the elite Draconis Combine regiment known as the Hikage, the Dragon's Shadow. Made up of primarily former Draconis Elite Strike Team operatives and DEST-trained MechWarriors, they were a select unit of troubleshooters serving under the direct command of *Gunji-no-Kanrei* Matsuhari Toranaga, House Kurita's Deputy of Military Affairs. The Hikage, along with the Fourth Dieron Regulars, had jumped into the system in response to Baxter's call, citing the relatively recent Unity Pact that bound the Draconis Combine and the Capellan Confederation against their collective enemies. While the Combine units had been quick to move into the system with their DropShips, they had so far not done anything to assist their Capellan allies or to strike at the Republic forces in any way.

Qiao quickly changed the subject. "Has the *gao-shiao-zhang* said anything about his plans when he returns?"

"Not yet, but I am sure he is coming up with something. Now that we have consolidated our forces, we are in the best possible position to deal with the Republic. Tara is as secure as we can make it, and with our DropShips now at Kohler Spaceport, we have a rapid means of relocation, should we need it." Lindsey was very careful not to put forth any theory of whom they might need to relocate from, but a quick glance at Qiao confirmed that she understood. "Now that you have set up this FOB, we can begin probing the Republic's weak points, preparing some punches of our own."

Qiao nodded, giving a predator's smile. The Republic forces had recently been using their newfound strength to conduct a series of raids on Capellan forces that had been stretched too thin in the wake of the disastrous battle at the Castle. The Capellans' Canopian allies, the First Canopian Lancers, had been particularly hard hit, their blockade of the Northwind Military Academy shattered by a series of hit-and-run strikes that had decimated the lighter forces. When the Highlanders reinforcements had moved to break the cordon around the NMA, the Canopian forces had been forced to retreat in good order, although not before they had suffered significant damage.

Despite the loss of the NMA, the Capellan task force was now in a far more solid tactical position. Having relinquished their hold on Kearney, all four of the Capellan-allied commands were now based out of Tara. The Canopians were taking advantage of the opportunity to rest and rearm under the safety provided by Warrior House Imarra and the Fourth McCarron's Armored Cavalry, while Laurel's Legion was prepared to strike where needed.

"Supposedly, the *gao-shiao-zhang* is bringing the local Maskirovka liaison back with him as well." A small flicker crossed Qiao's face, so quickly Lindsey thought she might have imagined it. "Hopefully he will have some additional information to give us."

Qiao gave a noncommittal nod, and Lindsey took a moment to consider what she had seen. The Maskirovka, the feared intelligence arm of the Capellan Confederation, was notorious for having assets in the most unlikely of places, and she had been unsurprised to find that at least one agent was permanently assigned to Northwind. While she had worked with intelligence liaisons before during her service with the Confederation, she had not had the opportunity to meet this particular agent until now. Maxwell Cheng, the author of several of the intelligence reports on her desk, had immediately attached himself to the *gao-shiao-zhang*'s staff on Kearney for the first portion of the campaign, citing the fact that Republic Knight Maeve Stirling had sent the bulk of her forces to such an unlikely location, believing it was part of a Republic plan to strike at their forces from an unexpected direction. Until now, Lindsey had rejoiced that she did not have to deal with the Capellan agent—she recalled vivid and unpleasant memories of other such minders in the past—but it seemed her good fortune had come to an end. "Is there something I should know?"

Despite them being alone, a knowing look in Qiao's expression confirmed discretion was the better part of valor. "I have not worked with him as much as the Grand Master has, but I found him quite zealous in the pursuit of the Confederation's objectives."

Lindsey knew she should maintain the same discretion, but was tempted to ask for more details. Qiao continued, however, quickly changing the topic. "Any chance we can make a few sorties before they return?" Lindsey gave a wan smile in reply. Qiao shook her head sadly. "I didn't think so."

"Don't worry, Julie," Lindsey replied, silently thanking Qiao for her tact. "You will get your chance at the action soon enough...sooner than I will, at least."

FIVE KILOMETERS WEST OF TARA
NORTHWIND
REPUBLIC OF THE SPHERE
4 DECEMBER 3150

"*Sang-wei*, I have something strange here."

In the cockpit of his *Shadow Hawk*, *Sang-wei* Thomas Han turned away from the late-night vista before him, glancing over to his comm board to verify which of his green MechWarriors had given the report. Ever since he had been given command of Charlie Lance, Han had been working hard to get to know the other members of his unit, but he still did not recognize their voices automatically. From the readout, he saw the transmission had come from Kenneth Turin, Charlie Three. The young man was considered something of a prodigy when it came to sensor systems, one of the reasons he had been assigned a *Raven* BattleMech in the Fourth McCarron's Armored Cavalry, allowing him to make the best use of his skills.

Unfortunately, Turin's appreciation for military-reporting etiquette still needed some work.

"I am going to need a bit more than that, MechWarrior Turin."

The younger man had the good sense to sound abashed. "Apologies, *Sang-wei*. I am getting an intermittent sensor signal from just outside the city gates. It's reading on mag-scan, but not on IR."

Han cycled through his own sensor suite to try picking up the anomalous reading, but wasn't surprised to find nothing. While his *Shadow Hawk* was considerably heavier than the *Raven* and provided the bulk of the firepower for the lance, its sensors did not have the range of the *Raven*'s.

"Enemy contacts?" Han asked, curiosity aroused despite himself. Rumors were the Republic forces were feeling bolder as of late, attempting to slip forces into the city under the cover of darkness since the failed attack on the Castle, but so far his lance had made no contact on their regular patrols.

Unfortunately, the majority of the intercepts so far had been made by the remaining Canopian forces *Sang-shao* Baxter had placed as a tripwire toward the city. While he understood the Canopians were better suited to the role with their lighter, faster BattleMechs, he still found it a bit galling to let the allied forces take on the bulk of the fighting for him.

For a moment, he considered holding position and calling the nearest Canopian detachment to check it out. He had already pushed his lance to the edge of their assigned patrol zone, but if there was a legitimate contact out there, he was well within his rights to check it out himself. Plus, he could deviate slightly from his patrol route far faster than it would take for the Canopians to arrive, so he quickly switched to the lance-wide comm channel.

"Charlie Two, Charlie Four, take flanking street and prepare for intercept. Charlie Three, you are with me." Han saw the *Raven* pilot following in his wake as Two and Four darted down the far street in their matched *Stinger*s. The paired light BattleMechs could quickly chase down any other 'Mechs they shook out of the underbrush, and he was confident his lance could handle anything long enough to call in reinforcements if needed.

Pressing out of the city limits, Han led the way, confident his *Shadow Hawk*'s heavier armor would protect him from any snipers in the area. The grassy plains leading into the distance were barely noticeable in the moonlight, shimmering in the breeze as approaching clouds darkened the sky even more. It had not snowed in several days, but a glance at the heavy gray tufts reminded him winter could strike hard and fast on Northwind—much like the native inhabitants.

"I'm not seeing anything, Three." Han's gaze roamed over the handful of warehouses and small farms on the city's outskirts. "Can you pin down a location?"

"No, sir," came Turin's nervous reply. "I'm sure I got something right around here, but the only things I'm seeing now are buildings and heavy equipment."

Han considered the situation a moment. If Republic troops were trying to make inroads into Tara following their recent consolidation of forces back at the Castle, this region would be a prime area to sneak through. It was primarily an agricultural and manufacturing region, which meant a minimum of bystanders would be present at this time of night, ensuring less chance of the Republic's movements being discovered. Of late, the greatest problem the Confederation troops faced was the massive perimeter they needed to patrol with limited resources, and the Republic forces knew that better than anyone.

The occasional times the Capellans had encountered Republic recon units had only worsened the situation. The night before, a Republic *Phoenix Hawk* had reached the outskirts of the city and devastated a Canopian *Wasp* before escaping into the darkness. Since then, all patrols had been in groups no smaller than lance strength, to ensure they were not challenged by superior tonnage and numbers, and so far there had been no further incidents.

A single day was hardly an impressive sample size, however.

"Two," Han said on the comm, "see if you can track them down. We'll cover you."

The *Stinger* pilot did not bother to confirm the order, merely shooting out of the city limits at full speed.

"No sign of anything... No, wait...residual heat signature..." There was a momentary pause from Two, and then his voice came back in a rush. "Contact! I have an unknown light 'Mech, hiding behind one of the warehouses."

"Got it!" Turin crowed. "I am reading it as a SDR-5V *Spider*."

That made sense, especially if the 'Mech belonged to the Highlanders' Grey Watch, the unit of older BattleMechs that had allegedly been secreted away on the planet in violation of Exarch Devlin Stone's 'Mech buyback program. The *Spider* was armed nearly as well as the two *Stingers* combined, but it was no match for Han's own 'Mech, or for the lance as a whole.

Han still did not see it on his own screens, but he did not doubt the identification. At the very least, the young *Stinger* pilot knew his way around his sensors. "Two, keep swinging around the long way, make sure they don't bolt back into the woods. Four, move up in support. I will block them on the far side. Three, you are my backstop."

He was not sure whether the active sensor scan or Two's maneuvers had tipped off the *Spider*, but the Gray Watch 'Mech's engine fired up from the low-power state it had been in to avoid detection. The *Spider* dashed around the far side of the building, away from the only threats in sight, the two Capellan *Stinger*s.

Right toward Han.

Han allowed himself a satisfied smile as he stepped out into the intersection, cutting off the *Spider* pilot's attempt to escape into the city. For a moment, he was ready for the *Spider* to jump over him, but Turin emerged from the shadows of a nearby building at the same time, ensuring he would not be caught that way.

The *Spider* pilot suddenly pulled back around the building, firing his two medium lasers at the closer of the pair of *Stinger*s. One beam clipped its right arm, but the other went wide, and Han could sense the Republic MechWarrior's desperation as the 'Mech backed up.

Rushing forward, he tried to put the *Spider* back under his guns, but the Republic BattleMech was already in a full-out sprint back toward the nearby farm, in search of a modicum of cover from the approaching Capellan forces.

The *Spider* backed up against a pair of stubby grain silos, painted crimson like the nearby barn itself. The pilot had to know they were trapped. The piles of wood and corrugated metal around the silos were too flimsy to provide cover for the upcoming onslaught, and the *Stinger*s were quickly closing from opposite directions to prevent any chance of escape.

Han stalked forward, his grin spreading across his face, his weapons charged and ready.

"*Sang*—" Three's voice cut in briefly, then died in a squeal of jamming.

Han's eyes immediately switched to the secondary monitor, where another pair of heat blooms had popped up onto his sensors, and he looked up to try locating the additional threat sources, the *Spider* now forgotten.

Were they hidden behind the grain silos? Han thought, only to be struck by a second, more urgent thought. *Weren't those silos facing the other way?*

By the time he recognized the "grain silos" were the source of the new sensor readings, the pair of squat *UrbanMech*s had already opened fire.

CHAPTER 2

"The first step toward victory is planning. The second is execution. The third is luck."

—Major Seamus Casey, Grey Watch, 13 June 3042

THE CASTLE
NORTHWIND
REPUBLIC OF THE SPHERE
5 DECEMBER 3150

Stepping quietly into the Castle's main conference room, Captain Declan Casey headed to an empty chair in the back, moving slowly to avoid drawing attention to himself. For this briefing, he wanted to be out from under the eyes of the command staff, far from the conference table at the front. Unlike the previous briefings he had attended here, this time the room seemed cavernously empty with only two handfuls of people occupying it.

From previous encounters with his commander, Brigadier General Luis McNamara, Declan knew he preferred using his office for a meeting this small, but with Countess Tara Campbell in attendance, certain courtesies needed to be maintained. From the look on the countess' face, she was thinking the same thing, although Declan had to admit it was a relief to pretend everything was as normal as she spoke softly with the general.

Despite being the shortest person around the table, the countess could not be mistaken for anything but a MechWarrior. The heavy fighting she had endured over the last several years barely seemed to have affected her outward appearance: she still kept her platinum-blond hair short and spiked, her fair complexion remained clear, and the only sign of the turmoil the Republic had endured was the occasional flash of sadness in her ice-blue eyes.

In contrast, the imposing Twelfth Hastati's commander could easily have been mistaken for a Clan Elemental. Even sitting, his broad, heavily muscled form squarely took up the center of the conference table, and a powerful fist tapped lightly on the tabletop that was nearly as dark as his own skin.

Aside from the general and the countess, the conference table also included the commanders of two of the other units from Terra, Colonel Yadira Alexandre of Stone's Defenders, and Colonel Thomas Palumbo of the Sixth Fides Defenders. The two made an unlikely pair, with the tall, willowy Alexandre standing out in sharp contrast to the stolid Palumbo, who seemed to share all of General McNamara's width but none of his height. A space remained for their executive officers, but most of them were clustered in the row of chairs at the front of the briefing room, allowing them to be seen without disrupting the flow from the unit commanders. Assorted off-duty lance and company commanders filled some of the raised seats in the briefing area, having received an open invitation to listen in on the recent update. Although the room was lightly occupied, enough people were present that Declan did not stand out among the attendees.

While listening to the meeting, he fidgeted with the knife Lady Maeve Stirling had given him. As a token of trust, he had exchanged knives with the Knight of the Republic more than a month ago, and whenever the future felt uncertain, he held onto the weapon as a reminder of the Republic's promise to protect the planet. He found himself regarding Maeve's blade more and more often of late.

When his grandfather, Seamus Casey, collapsed heavily into the adjacent seat, Declan nearly dropped the knife in surprise, but caught it before it could hit the floor.

"Still in the doghouse?" Seamus said. The burly Highlander was dressed in black jeans and a heavy woolen sweater, but his body language still said "MechWarrior."

"Apparently so," Declan replied, catching a studiously neutral glance from General McNamara. During the Capellan attack on the Castle, Declan had refused to retreat as ordered, and while his decision to stay had been instrumental in ensuring the Grey Watch survived until the Republic reinforcements arrived, the general had been quick to show his displeasure. While the Twelfth Hastati Sentinels needed all of the soldiers they could muster right now, Declan had no doubt he was deep in the doghouse, and that a reckoning would be coming when the crisis had passed.

Across the table, Lady Maeve Stirling, the Knight of the Sphere who had been sent from Terra to assist in the defense of Northwind, noticed him as she took her own seat at the front of the room, and sent Declan a quick but reassuring smile that he returned just as swiftly. She was one of the last Republic unit commanders last to arrive, having just returned from Kearney with the survivors of the force she had originally brought to Northwind. Her company had been instrumental in retaking Fort Barrett, and now she and her troops had returned to the Castle to rest and rearm while the duty of holding the fort now fell to the detachment of Stone's Defenders.

Seamus chuckled. "Well, it seems not everyone is displeased with ye," he said, running a free hand through his bushy gray beard.

Declan studiously ignored his grandfather and quickly changed the subject. "I heard about the grain solo trap... Who'd have thought an *UrbanMech* could do so much damage?"

Seamus glanced over at his grandson, his expression uncharacteristically serious. "Dinna knock the *Urbie*, Dec. It may not be the fastest BattleMech out there, or the most nimble, but it knows how to get the job done."

Declan nodded slowly—all he would do to apologize in this situation—and switched subjects again. "Why aren't you up there? I'm sure Colonel Griffin wants you at his side."

Colonel Michael Griffin, the commander of the Grey Watch, the previously concealed regiment of the fabled Northwind Highlanders mercenaries, was seated at the table with the other commanders. His XO, Lieutenant Colonel Cadha Jaffray, was out in the field.

"This is exactly where I'm supposed to be, lad," Seamus replied. "And dinna ye forget it."

Declan gave the elder man a brief smile, but his gaze went toward the entrance as another latecomer came in at the far end of the room. Lieutenant Colonel Joseph Halloran sat down in the back without acknowledging anyone else.

"Apparently, ye are not the only one in the doghouse," Seamus replied, giving Halloran a small nod, which he either ignored or did not see.

"What happened?" Declan asked, unable to stifle his curiosity. "Surely they don't blame him for the Canopian siege on the NMA?"

Halloran was the senior instructor at the Northwind Military Academy, which had been besieged by the First Canopian Lancers, the Capellans' allies from the Magistracy of Canopus. Like several of the other instructors, he had remained behind, giving most of the younger soldiers the opportunity to escape, but a core of talented cadets and hardened veterans under his command had managed to keep the Canopians from taking the facility. The mysterious Grey Watch unit had made their first appearance during that initial battle, and had been instrumental in ensuring that the NMA did not fall. The Grey Watch had recently fought a second battle at the NMA, forcing the Canopians into a rapid withdrawal.

"No one knows. He's been sour ever since he returned...more sour than usual." Seamus shook his head. "I suppose we canna blame him for bein' a little off. We're all to be feelin' it."

Declan nodded, having thought the same thing himself. Ever since the Capellan forces had struck at the Highlanders' homeworld, the defenders of Northwind had fought a series of desperate battles to protect their home and maintain control of the planet's hyperpulse generator, one of the rare few functioning HPG stations left in the Inner Sphere—a priceless strategic asset whose value could not be ignored.

The Twelfth Hastati, the Republic's garrison force on Northwind, had fought valiantly against overwhelming odds, but everyone in the room knew their recent success had been thanks to the arrival of reinforcements, both new and old.

The old had been the reveal of the Grey Watch, the secret Highlanders unit created decades ago to defend Northwind if it should become necessary. While Declan was still sore at his grandfather for never telling him such a unit existed, the Grey Watch had provided experienced pilots and additional

BattleMechs at a vital moment in the planet's defense, and he certainly could not argue with their results.

The new had been the arrival of Countess Tara Campbell, riding to the rescue with both her own Highlanders battalion and two formations of Republic troops, shattering the Capellans' final push against the Castle, the Hastati's final redoubt against the Capellan attackers. The hellish battle had taken a heavy toll on both sides, with the Republic forces holding the base and the Capellan forces being pushed back to the city of Tara to lick their wounds.

Under regular circumstances, the Republic forces would have followed up with a quick riposte into Tara, to force the wounded Capellan troops to either protect the HPG compound or fall back and regroup.

Unfortunately, these were anything but normal circumstances. Before the Republic forces could capitalize on their gains, a second set of JumpShips had jumped into the system. Reinforcements for the Capellans had arrived, but not in the form anyone could have expected: troops from the Draconis Combine.

Under the terms of the relatively new Unity Pact between the two nations, the militaries of both the Capellan Confederation and Draconis Combine could work together on planned operations, but no one had expected Combine forces to appear in the Northwind system. The Republic troops had been forced to consolidate their gains before the Draconis forces came in-system on a small flotilla of DropShips. Whereas a quick attack to throw the Capellans off balance would have been the smartest tactical move earlier, it might bog the Republic forces down in enemy territory and leave them vulnerable for the Combine troops to drop into their rear areas.

However, there were also signs that the Capellans were just as surprised as the Republic was by House Kurita's arrival. From what Republic intelligence had gathered, the terms of the Unity Pact were notoriously vague over joint operations, and both the timing of the Kuritans' appearance and their curious actions since jumping in-system had raised several eyebrows in the Republic camp. Instead of landing on the planet and immediately going on the offensive, the Combine forces had remained in geosynchronous orbit, prepared to drop down at a multitude of vectors, allowing them to come down on top of the Castle, Fort Barrett, or Tara at will. However, as of yet, they had done nothing at all.

Seeing that everyone had arrived, General McNamara graciously gestured at the countess, allowing her to take the lead in the meeting. Despite him being the senior military officer for the planet, both the countess' bloodline and her recent mandate from the Exarch of the Republic made him happy to allow her to take on the burden of command.

Tara Campbell's smile and nod to him was equally cordial. She then turned to Colonel Alexandre. "Colonel, can you give us an update on the current status of the Castle?"

"Of course, ma'am." The gentle lilt of Alexandre's English accent was strangely calming in the face of impending danger. "With the general's consent, Stone's Defenders have taken over the primary defensive responsibilities for both the Castle and Fort Barrett, using a variation of the defensive planning the Hastati used during the last battle. Currently, we have provided a multilayered defense using our BattleMech assets, with armor and infantry elements securing the immediate perimeter and various entranceways. At this time, my staff feels confident we can repulse any attack short of full regimental strength."

Declan nodded, seeing the wisdom of allowing Alexandre to lead the defense. Stone's Defenders were known as the premier defensive regiment in Stone's Brigade, and they drilled regularly for exactly this sort of mission. Equipped with a variety of heavy and superheavy BattleMechs, such as the *Ares* OmniMechs, they were far from the most nimble of forces, but they could field a withering amount of firepower. Although Stone's Defenders were rarely deployed as the tip of the spear, when Devlin Stone ordered something to be held, the Defenders were the ones to do it.

If Colonel Alexandre said she and her forces could hold, they would hold.

"Excellent, Colonel. My compliments to your team," the countess replied. "With that in mind, it looks like we are ready to move on to planning for the assault on the city. General, would you bring us up to speed on your efforts?"

"Thank you, Countess," McNamara responded. "With the Defenders taking over the protection of the Castle, and with your forces ensuring that we are prepared to move forward, I released two companies' worth of light units to scout the city's outskirts and provide updated reconnaissance."

He glanced over at the young officer who sat behind the console that controlled the monitors on the far wall. The displays illuminated with recorded stills cut from BattleMech battleROM footage. "The Capellans are running patrols with their light units, and have blocked all of the main arterials into Tara proper. Any attempt to breach the barricades would have to be done with significant resources, which would potentially bog us down in a block-by-block fight. While I might have risked it before the Kuritan forces arrived, we risk being crushed against the Capellans if the Kuritans should make a combat drop against us."

"Is that likely?" Colonel Palumbo asked. "They have made no moves to land so far."

The general shrugged a shoulder. "I do not know about likely, Colonel, but from their orbital positioning they have the option to drop on us at any time, which means we have to factor it into our planning. While we do not know the specifics of the current agreement between the Capellans and the Kuritans, we do know that they are officially allied under the Unity Pact, which lends a certain level of concern that they might strike at us under a single unified banner.

"Unfortunately, the Kuritans are not the only ones we have to worry about. While we have been resting and rearming, the Capellan forces have also been busy. They have abandoned Fort Barrett on Kearney and brought all of their forces to Tara, going so far as to land their DropShips at the spaceport. The additional forces mean they can increase patrols around the city, and they have consolidated their hold to make it easier to defend. There are also signs that they have set up a forward operating base somewhere between Tara and the Castle, but we have not determined where yet. Unfortunately, our traditional aerial recon options have become very limited. The Capellans took great pains to sweep our reconnaissance satellites from orbit before their drop, and they have seeded the area between Tara and the Castle with anti-aircraft units to discourage recon flights. With our aerial forces already severely depleted in the wake of the recent battle, I have decided to hold off on revealing our additional aerial recon assets until absolutely required."

"Agreed. I believe you also mentioned earlier that you have sent ground patrols to try locating the FOB, General?" the Countess asked.

McNamara nodded. "We do, but we have been forced to operate in lances due to the Capellans' electronic warfare capabilities. Their *Ravens* can spot us as we approach, and it is vital for our units to have sufficient strength to either attack or disengage once we find them. That, unfortunately, has been slowing our efforts."

"Well done, General. Please let us know when we have any more information on their location. How are repairs progressing?"

"Both the Twelfth and the Grey Watch took serious damage during the defense of the Castle," McNamara responded. "We have managed to alleviate some of our losses with battlefield salvage, but there are still some parts we need. Currently, we are able to field several companies each, and we should be ready to fight within the next eighteen hours."

"Very good," Tara replied. "Colonel Griffin, do you have anything to add?"

"Yes, Countess," Griffin replied. "The Grey Watch was primarily established in a cell structure to maintain operational security, which allowed us to remain undetected before we revealed ourselves to break the siege of the Northwind Military Academy. One of the ways we managed to do that was by spreading out our cells throughout the continent, mostly centered on Tara for logistical reasons. However, due to a number of factors, not the least of which being the speed in which we were forced to muster, several of our cells could not link up with us before we broke out from Tara. I have dispatched messages to several units that were unable to break away at the beginning of the conflict, and they have responded. Technically, that means we have several lances behind enemy lines."

"You have forces *in* Tara?" the general asked incredulously.

"We do, but not as many as we could have hoped," Griffin replied. "The majority were BattleMechs that would not have made it to the Castle's defense in time, and MechWarriors who refused to abandon their homes for one reason or another. I made the decision to keep them where they were for now, knowing that we might need them later on, but communications have been spotty at best."

"Can they help us with an attack plan for the city?"

"I certainly believe so, now that we have reestablished communications, but we need to make sure they remain secure. I have some of my best people on it right now, and I hope to hear from them shortly."

"Very well, Colonel. Anything else?"

"Just the reminder that the Grey Watch is with you, ma'am, all the way. We always knew we might someday be called on to deal with another threat to Northwind, and we are ready to kick the Cappies right off our planet."

The countess smiled thinly, and then nodded. "As always, Colonel, you provide me with new hope when things look their darkest. Do we have any other questions to get out of the way before we plan our next steps?"

The general's expression hardened, and he looked carefully at the countess. "I know this is the last question any of us want to ask, but I feel it is my responsibility to do so..."

Tara raised a hand to stop him, preventing further discomfort. "I know exactly what you are going to ask, General. Unfortunately, I am sorry to say that I see no possibility of additional reinforcements coming from Terra."

Colonel Griffin's expression mirrored McNamara's. "Even though we are now besieged from two directions, putting not one but two enemies on the Republic's doorstep?"

"Even if we were besieged from ten directions," she replied solemnly. "Even though that is how it must feel of late. Unfortunately, it's a matter of resources, and the Republic's are extremely limited right now. Not only did the Exarch send what he could, I am convinced he sent us with more than he could safely spare, and that was only to hold up one end of a covenant he made a long time ago. The Republic simply has nothing more available." She looked around the room carefully. "I know this the last thing that anyone wants to hear, but we are going to have to fight this battle ourselves."

"As we shall, ma'am," the general replied with equal solemnity, returning the focus of the room.

Declan noticed Maeve making a show of rubbing her face, covering the small smile that threatened to escape. She was clearly enjoying how deftly the situation had been handled. He wondered if Tara and McNamara might have staged the question for the benefit of the other commanders, and this way they were able to speak with a single voice.

"Do you want to share your thoughts on our mission planning?" the general continued.

"I believe they will do best to hear it from you, General," Tara replied. "You were the heart and soul of it, after all."

For the briefest of moments, McNamara straightened slightly at her praise, like a newly minted cadet. He gestured to his aide, who put an aerial view of the region up on the monitors; taken from a variety of orbiting satellites, the image focused on the Castle and the city of Tara. "Currently, we are trying to focus on our advantages, namely our familiarity with the area, and the many watchful eyes that are on our side in the city. While the Capellan forces have blocked many of the civilian channels and set up jammers between the city and here, we are still receiving some intelligence from a variety of sources. Our most up-to-date intel tells us the Capellans are maintaining patrols throughout the city, but are keeping a relatively light hand otherwise. One of our greatest concerns was that they would act brutally toward our friends and family in Tara, which would have put us in a difficult position.

"With that being the case, we currently have two mutual goals, aside from our continued defense of the Castle. As Colonel Griffin mentioned earlier, he is working with his Grey Watch forces to establish a foothold in the city, potentially to spur a resistance movement that can assist us when the time is right to take retake the city..."

At the general's nod, Griffin picked up the thread. "We are also providing a final line of defense for the people of Tara. The Capellans are not known for their restraint, and several of my troops wanted to provide a firebreak should things get bad. Beyond that, we have been using probing forces to see if we can pull some of their patrols out of position. We managed to get one or two of their younger MechWarriors to extend out a bit too far, but they've wised up since then."

"What are you hoping to gain?" Colonel Alexandre asked.

Griffin smiled. "I am hoping they fail to notice that some of the 'Mechs attacking them are not coming from the outside, nor are they returning to the Castle. We have already snuck some additional 'Mechs into the city under the noses of their patrols, but it is getting harder to move in anything larger than 50 tons. When the balloon finally goes up, our goal is to try to hit them from more directions than they can deal with. Due to the sheer scope of the space they are trying to cover, and the confining nature of the city streets, they are forced to spread out while sweeping the city's outskirts. Our maneuverability and familiarity with the terrain gives us a major advantage, and the fact that many of the people of Tara want to openly help us is giving us a much better picture of what is going on there."

"Thank you, Colonel," the general said. "However, Tara is just one of our targets. I believe our greater concern must be the Capellan staging area we believe is outside the city limits. When they do decide to strike at us again, the threat will undoubtedly come from there."

Declan nodded again. Until now, the Capellans had been focused on maintaining their hold on the city, specifically the HPG compound. If they were setting up a forward operating base, it would either be to intercept any strikes on the city at a distance, or to provide a staging area for a new strike on the Castle.

Maeve leaned forward, looking directly at the Highlanders' commander. "Countess, have we attempted to reach out to the Combine forces?"

Tara smiled back at her. "We are of the same mind, Lady Maeve. I was planning on having the general reach out to the Combine commander immediately following the meeting."

"The general?" Maeve asked, surprised. "Not yourself?"

Once again the countess smiled. "Let's not show our cards immediately. As the official military commander for the Republic forces on Northwind, I believe General McNamara will be able to get further with him than I would... but if the Combine wants to speak to me, it knows where to find me."

She turned back to the table as a whole. "You have cut to the heart of the matter. Knowing exactly what the Kuritans are looking for will be vital to planning our next steps."

"Do you think they want the HPG for themselves?" Maeve asked.

The countess shrugged eloquently. "I don't know what to think yet. The fact they have not made planetfall is a curious aspect. Not only that, the composition of their force is telling: I believe this might be everything the

Combine could spare on short notice, and that may mean their goals are far more limited and short-term than their Capellan counterparts.' The Capellans came loaded for bear, seeking to hold the entire planet. I am fairly sure the Kuritan goals are far more modest."

Or targeted, Declan thought, seeing the same things the Countess did. As with everything, it paid to watch the fault lines.

Tara Campbell's cool gaze swept around the room. "Are there any other questions?"

No one else spoke, and everyone was carefully dismissed. Maeve hung back, waiting to speak to the countess and the general, and joined them on their side of the table.

"Well, that was interestin'," Seamus said, standing with a stretch. "Always good for us to know where we stand. Where are ye off to now?"

"Thought I'd check to see how the technicians are doing on my 'Mech, and then potentially spend a couple hours in the simulator. What about you?"

"Canna interest ye in something a li'l different?" Seamus asked.

Declan looked over at him suspiciously. "Like what?"

"I received a message from a couple of old friends shortly before the meeting, and I thought about taking a ride. Care to come?"

CHAPTER 3

"A mandatory curfew will be imposed in the city of Tara from 9 p.m. to 7 a.m. local. Travel during these times will be highly restricted. Only essential workers holding a signed necessity pass will be allowed to travel via the following routes..."

—Official Capellan Confederation press release
to all news outlets, 5 December 3150

OUTSKIRTS OF TARA
NORTHWIND
REPUBLIC OF THE SPHERE
5 DECEMBER 3150

Declan Casey swore bitterly as the jeep he was riding in struck another bump. He yearned to rub his hands together to warm them, but he was too busy using them to hold onto his seat. The bitter breeze cut right through the heavy fabric of his pants, although the heavy wool expedition jacket he wore kept his torso comfortable. Behind the wheel, his Seamus Casey laughed harshly, reveling in his grandson's discomfort.

I suppose I deserve that... Declan thought, not blaming his grandfather one bit. He had been sour company the entire way in, but regretted attempting to make this very unofficial covert insertion into the city instead of being out in the field with his lance.

Despite his initial interest in accompanying his grandfather, the long, silent drive had only allowed him to brood. Declan did not regret anything he had done...much. During the battle at the Castle, his unit had been ordered to retreat back inside the wall of the fortress while members of the Grey Watch gave them cover, willingly sacrificing themselves to allow the Twelfth Hastati's more advanced BattleMechs to live another day. One of Declan's lancemates had broken formation and went to help, and she had been killed before the rest of his lance could support her. His remaining lancemates had stood with him and the Grey Watch 'Mechs, ready to sacrifice all as well...until the Republic reinforcements had arrived, saving them all from certain death.

The arrival of Countess Tara Campbell had done nothing to save him from the consequences of his decision to ignore orders, however. His BattleMech, a *Marauder II*, had taken heavy damage during the battle, and while he was sure the general would not have intentionally dropped him to the very bottom of the repair queue during a war, he'd seen his lance temporarily split up while his company was reorganized to deal with the losses from the Capellan assault. Instead of deploying with them, he'd spent most of his time helping the technicians repair other BattleMechs or assisting in training some of the younger warriors, all of whom were becoming veterans far too quickly for his liking.

When his grandfather had asked him to come on a special mission for Colonel Griffin, he had been thrilled to have something else to do. He quickly received permission from the general to accompany his grandfather—almost too quickly, as if McNamara was silently glad to be rid of him for a few days—and they had set out in the dead of night to sneak into the city.

"Ye dinna have to come with me, ye know!" the elder Casey said, making a vain attempt to conceal a grin by running his free hand through his beard. "Corvin woulda been just as happy to ride shotgun!"

Declan glanced into the back seat, where William Corvin sat sideways on the rear seat, his long legs locking him into position to keep a close watch on their rear. The powerfully built infantryman was an old friend of Seamus', and he did indeed have an old-fashioned automatic shotgun close at hand. Declan had been initially concerned that having the weapon in the vehicle would tip off any Capellan patrols as to their identity, but the reality was most inhabitants of Northwind went around armed, especially in the harsh winter months when local predators extended their hunting zones. Not to mention, as Seamus had said, if a Capellan patrol got close enough to spot the shotgun, things had probably already gone horribly wrong.

Corvin smiled at him grimly, then turned back to the rear window. They had been running silent and without lights, but had finally reached the outskirts of the city. This was the most daunting part, breaching the perimeter at a point where Seamus' contacts had informed him about a gap in the Capellans' patrol schedule.

Seamus stopped the vehicle under a snow-covered overhang next to an all-night restaurant that had been closed due to the curfew the Capellan overlords had mandated, then quickly turned off the engine and waited. They had received excellent intelligence on the timing of the patrols in the area, and Seamus knew how best to take advantage of such information.

They waited several minutes, and were rewarded by the sight of a Tamerlane strike sled through the alleyway as it went through its patrol sweep, its turreted medium laser at the ready as it searched for targets. The fleet little hovertank moved quickly, and Declan found himself unconsciously holding his breath as he waited for them to be discovered.

Seamus gave the scout several minutes to clear the area, then grinned at his companions and gunned the engine to head deeper into the city. It took them only ten more minutes to reach their destination, with Seamus pulling into a private garage.

A single glance at their location allowed Declan to understand why his grandfather had asked him to come. "Plunkett's?"

Seamus smiled as he closed the garage door. "Where else? I've been feeling a bit parched."

The three men carefully crept down the alley, ensuring they kept to the sidewalk rather than showing footprints in the snow, and carefully checked for any other vehicles before crossing the street to the back entrance of the famed Highlanders bar.

After pulling a key from his pocket, Seamus let them into the bar's back entrance. "It is good to have friends, int it?"

Corvin glanced at him, giving him a slightly arch look. "I'll keep an eye out here. Be ready to move."

"Ye've got it," Seamus replied, handing him the key. "Dinna get caught."

The infantryman smiled, the expression all teeth, and then stepped back out into the cold. Seamus made sure that the door was secure before heading into the next room.

Two men and a woman already occupied it, all of whom Declan knew. Francis "Tux" Tuxberious smiled from the far end of the bar, leaning forward on his barstool, a half-full beer glass in front of him. The youngest in the room, he gave off an air of practiced nonchalance. Only someone who had seen him at the controls of his *Wolverine* would know the man was a little bit nuts, always willing to do the wild thing to make an effect. The frustrating thing was that his approach worked more often than not, which was the only reason he hadn't been benched long ago. Such antics were more the realm of Solaris arena fighters, not the Northwind Highlanders, but no one could doubt Tux's effectiveness.

The woman in the room was Cathy Glazier, who stood quickly and give Declan a hug with a strength that belied her advanced years. While the gray-haired woman in front of him could have been mistaken as his own grandmother—especially in the deft way she studiously ignored his grandfather—Declan knew she was a crafty tactician and a damned fine MechWarrior.

The third occupant was a slight surprise, although he shouldn't have been: Danny, the owner of Plunkett's, was a former MechWarrior who had suffered from extensive neuroshock on a drop. The powerful man still walked with a limp, but Declan always had thought that more of an affection than a true injury, having seen the man move like lightning when dealing with rowdy patrons.

As usual, Seamus was the first to speak. "Well now, isnae this a sorry group?"

"You should talk, Seamus Casey," Cathy replied, turning to him for the first time. "Took you long enough to finally get here." She glanced over at Declan. "At least you brought someone with a proper appreciation for good company!"

Declan smiled, but Seamus cut him off before he could say anything. "And where the hell were ye when we were pulling out of the city? Did ye stay out too late for a pint that night?"

Cathy glared at him, but a twinkle in her eye said she was just being ornery for the sake of it. "Tux left a shepherd's pie in the oven. He had to go back for it."

Seamus shook his head, ready to say something more, but Cathy cut him off, her voice suddenly more serious than Declan ever remembered hearing it. "There were Capellan troops in my granddaughter's neighborhood, Seamus. I couldnae leave."

Seamus looked from Cathy to Tux, who nodded. After a moment, he shook his head, whatever he meant to say forgotten. "Where are Darryl and Scott? I would think they'd be here with ye."

"On their way back," Cathy replied. "You heard about that little to-do with the *UrbanMech*s? I sent the two of 'em ta back up Joe Tilly's lance. The wee devils did a good job, but I wanted to make sure they had some cover if the Cappies got to 'em more quickly than we expected. They're takin' the long route home ta avoid detection."

This time, Seamus did crack a smile. "I shoulda known." He took a seat at the bar and gestured for Declan to do the same, turning towards the other three as he settled. "We only have a wee bit of time if we are going to avoid the patrol shift change on our way back. What's going on?"

Danny spoke up now that the tense moment had passed. "We have some information the countess has to hear, and soon. First and foremost, the Capellans are beginning a major redeployment. I've a few friends in the independent repair trade, and from what they're hearing, the Cappies are nearly back up to fighting strength. They moved on to repairing the Canopians' equipment about three days ago."

Seamus nodded. If the Canopians were now top priority for repairs, it meant the Capellans were ready for a fight. While they certainly could not have replaced all of their losses, the invaders would at least be in a good enough position to strike out from the city. "Do we know how soon they're going to move?"

"Not yet, but I'd say less than a week. They're reinforcing all along their lines, but we're seeing some holes where they are starting to scale down. They are definitely getting ready for a push."

"Any thoughts where that push might be?"

Cathy leaned against the bar thoughtfully. "If you're asking my opinion, I would guess another strike at the NMA." The Northwind Military Academy had been under heavy siege from Capellan and Canopian forces when the invasion first began, but the arrival of Republic reinforcements had broken the stalemate, bringing most of the Capellan troops back into the safety of the city, where the Highlanders would be hesitant to cause damage.

"Do they really think they can make any headway against the campus now?" Declan asked, thinking about Halloran and his grim expression from the briefing earlier.

"Not a chance in hell," Cathy responded. "Still, the fact that they were doing it would mean you'd have to devote some sort of resources to help defend it. That's why I think they'll be using the Magistracy troops: if we push back too hard, the Capellans will not be too devastated by the losses, but the

Canopians are light and fast enough to disengage as necessary. If the fight for the breakout turns too terrible, the Capellans can either block off any assistance from the NMA or join the fight with a flanking maneuver. Either one would work well for them."

Declan nodded, seeing the sense of the attack plan. The First Canopian Lancers were the lightest invading units on the field, and while they had taken damage during the siege of the NMA and the attack on the Castle, they still remained a very potent force.

"Do you have any resources here we can use to disrupt them?" Seamus asked.

"A couple companies," Cathy replied, "but most are positioned to protect the residential sector of the district—at least that we are sure of. A few of our fellow warriors failed to report in, and we're still trying to be cautious about reaching out to them. If the Maskirovka is on to them, we do not want the trail to lead back to us. Still, when we are needed, we'll be able to bring some more firepower into the fight."

Seamus nodded, although Declan saw the sad edge to his expression. While Cathy's absence had been deeply missed on the battlefield during the defense of the Castle, Declan could tell Seamus was a bit jealous that they were preparing to protect their homes the best way they knew how.

"Okay, we can get this information back to the countess immediately, but I'm still not sure why ye needed us here, personally. We're not bloody couriers. Ye coulda sent a message."

For a moment, Cathy and Tux looked a little guilty, and their gaze fell on Danny as the bartender finally spoke up. "That was for me, I am afraid. I am hoping you can pull me out tonight when you get out of here. I've...been forced to temporarily close the bar."

"What happened?"

"Yer gal happened," Danny replied, giving Declan a smile. "She came in the other day looking for ye."

"Bianca?" Declan tried to conceal his surprise, hoping his concern did not give him away. Over the last few days he had buried himself in his duties to keep from thinking about his friend, who had been unable to contact him due to the communications jamming the Capellans had seeded throughout the city. Bianca Haller was a ComStar researcher for Project Sunlight, the Republic's effort to fix the persistent malfunctions plaguing the HPGs in the interstellar communications network. Her vital research was meant to help end the Blackout that began almost two decades ago, but the Capellans' capture of the HPG had halted her team's progress.

Danny nodded. "She apparently made quite a few friends in a very short time, and the Capellans have been giving her the freedom to leave the HPG compound from time to time, to retrieve food and run similar errands. The staff's been getting tired of rations, and they won't let anyone they don't know into the compound. Bianca's been careful to split things up between a few different places, but when she comes here, she drops off some choice information."

Declan smiled brightly, but the expression froze when he saw Danny's expression turn grim. "The last time she was here, however, she came to see if she could find you, and to warn you that we were both compromised."

"What happened?" Declan asked, his fingers digging into the bartop.

Danny shook his head. "She suspected it had something to do with the new Maskirovka liaison. *Sang-shao* Baxter, the Fourth MAC's commander, seemed to trust Bianca, but the liaison, an Agent Cheng, seems just as suspicious as the rest of his people."

"Could they be watching this place?" Seamus asked, his eyes flicking to the door, but Danny put up a cautious hand.

"We have some people in the area. We'll know if anyone moves anywhere near us, and we've already compromised most of the surveillance devices focused here. We knew before they came to pick me up."

"How did ye get out?" Seamus asked.

"I was lucky enough to not be here... It was Wednesday, my haircut day. Evan was working the bar, and he let me know. They've been looking for me, but I knew where to bolt to."

Declan remained focused on what Danny had already said. "What about Bianca? Won't they think she betrayed them?"

"She's one hell of a wee lass," Danny said with a smile. "She's confident she can make them think you just bolted off with the information, don't ask me how. Regardless, we'll want to do something for her when we can."

Declan nodded. "Did she say anything else?"

Cathy took up the tale from there. "Yes, and that's the kicker: from what we have heard, there may be no love lost between the Cappies and our new Drac visitors."

That managed to pull Declan out of his reverie. "What?"

"Supposedly, the weather is a little icy between the two forces, if you get my meaning. They seem mighty concerned that the Kuritans are talking to yon countess for one, and the fact they haven't yet landed to support the Capellans isn't going over well in the Capellan camp."

Declan gave a small, thoughtful nod, but Seamus leaned forward, glancing between the two of them. "But dinna they call for the Kuritans?"

"They sent out a call for reinforcements, didn't specify from where. I think they only expected other Cappies would step in. From what Bianca was able to read between the lines, Baxter thinks this is an independent operation by the Drac commander. You know how these Dracs are—all about honor and face and initiative."

"So they are thinking the Kuritans—"

"Are potentially here to steal their prize out from under their very noses," Danny responded with a tight grin. "Now, don't that beat all?"

"That makes for a very interesting bit of news to get back to the countess." Seamus nodded sharply. "We'll definitely take ye back, Danny, but is the rest of yer staff gonna be all right?"

"We'll take care of them," Tux replied. "The Maskirovka is good, but we have a few tricks they don't know about... We're ready to move if there is an issue."

Declan felt somewhat comforted by the information, but was unable to forget the main question on his mind. "Are we going to do anything about Bianca?" he asked, hastily adding, "And the rest of the ComStar researchers?"

"From what yon lass had said, she's doing fine at the moment," Danny replied. "The Capellans need them ta work the HPG station, and as long as they don't put up any sort of resistance, they're being left alone. They lost some of their security forces in the original scuffle, but we managed to get a few of the others out during the fray. We have good intel on the compound, and we should be able to sneak in there when we need ta."

Declan nodded, the first threads of a plan already forming in his mind, and his grandfather gave a telling smile before turning back to the others.

"Okay, we'll roll out and get this intel back to the countess," Seamus said. "Anything else we can do ta make yer lives a little easier?"

"A few more companies causing some havoc would not be missed," Cathy replied, and Tux nodded at that as well.

Wishing them both farewell, Seamus patted them both on the back, and the two Caseys headed back into the main room with Danny before stepping out into the night. All three men loaded up into the jeep, careful to keep quiet, while Corvin sauntered back out of the shadows.

"Any problems?" Declan asked the infantryman, noticing a small fleck of blood on his cheek.

Corvin shook his head. "Couple of street thugs, thought we might not be missing our ride. I convinced them I was not the man they were looking to deal with tonight."

"As long as ye did it quietly," Seamus replied, and Corvin replied with another smile that was all teeth.

Declan nodded, keeping his thoughts to himself as Corvin swung up into the vehicle and Seamus revved up the engine. Moments later, they were headed down the street, their tracks covered by the blowing snow, rushing back out into the night.

CHAPTER 4

"Early reports state that Capellan forces have departed Kearney, moving the bulk of the occupying forces to the city of Tara. We can only speculate whether this is related to the failed strike on the Castle, or whether this is a prelude to a new front for the ongoing conflict."

—Tegan Shea, *Northwind News*, 7 December 3150

HPG COMPOUND
TARA, NORTHWIND
REPUBLIC OF THE SPHERE
7 DECEMBER 3150

Sang-shao Lindsey Baxter stood stiffly in front of Northwind's HPG station, the cold breeze nothing compared to the harsh chill she felt within as she awaited the arrival of *Gao-shiao-zhang* Jiang Hui.

No matter how hard she tried, she could not shake the feeling that she had failed. When the Capellan forces first invaded the Republic planet of Northwind, her Fourth McCarron's Armored Cavalry had quickly taken the city and its true prize: one of the few working HPG stations left, the key to rapid communications between worlds. As a reward for succeeding on the main objective of their mission, she had been tasked with defending the site against counterattacks by Republic forces, while the rest of the Capellan forces defended the less vital locations they had captured.

Unfortunately, such targets were becoming few and far between. The siege of the Northwind Military Academy, maintained by elements of Colonel Centrella-Tompkins' First Canopian Lancers, had been broken, causing the remaining allied forces to retreat back into the city limits. With her primary skirmisher force damaged, Lindsey had been forced to redistribute her own forces, which had forced *Gao-shiao-zhang* Hui, her tacit superior, to adjust his own tactical planning.

Originally, Warrior House Imarra had paired itself with Laurel's Legion, allowing Lindsey's regiment to operate alone, without Hui's supervision. She had seen this autonomy as a compliment, with Hui showing his faith in her abilities in the early phases of the invasion as he oversaw the less-experienced regiment while invading the continent of Kearney.

Unfortunately, the rumors of secret stores of Republic personnel and materiel on Kearney seemed unfounded, and her fellow Capellans had found nothing but a guerrilla force left behind to harass them. The remaining Republic troops had taunted them like a picador, causing tiny wounds that amounted to little in and of themselves, but goading their larger prey into making a potentially fatal mistake.

The loss of the NMA had wound up being the final straw for the *gao-shiao-zhang*. With one of his units seriously damaged, and new Republic reinforcements consolidating on New Lanark, the primary continent, Hui had made the difficult decision to consolidate his forces at the HPG and the city of Tara. Moving swiftly, Warrior House Imarra's leader had boarded his troops on their DropShips, while Laurel's Legion carefully destroyed anything the Republic might try to use when they retook Fort Barrett.

Their tasks completed, the Capellan forces had moved to Kohler Spaceport under the cover of darkness. Laurel's Legion had established a forward staging area outside the city limits, and Warrior House Imarra had bolstered the Fourth MAC within the city itself.

Despite knowing it was the correct strategic decision, Lindsey could not help but see it as a rebuke, a response to her own failure. Her task had been to keep the continent secure, and despite her best efforts, she had been unable to blunt the Republic threat. Her attack against the Castle had come so close to breaking the back of the Republic defenses on New Lanark, but unfortunately, her plans had been for naught. The Republic forces, aided by a previously unknown Northwind Highlanders unit known as the Grey Watch, had repelled her efforts to take the Castle, and had stymied her efforts just long enough for Republic reinforcements to arrive from Terra, led by none other than Countess Tara Campbell.

The arrival of the unexpected Republic troops had been the death knell for Lindsey's hopes for a quick victory. Facing fresh Republic forces bearing down on her and with her own units running low on armor and ammunition, she had been forced to pull back to the city to prepare for the inevitable counterattack. Following a conversation with the *gao-shiao-zhang*, she had sent an urgent HPG message requesting reinforcements, compounding her shame as she had to admit an inability to complete her mission despite their earlier victories.

To add insult to injury, her reinforcements had come not from the Confederation, but from a wholly unexpected direction: soldiers of the Draconis Combine Mustered Soldiery, allies from the Unity Pact, which had jumped into the system upon receiving her message and immediately burned for the planet with a flotilla of DropShips. She knew that only the threat of these new arrivals kept the Republic from pushing back into the city, and she loathed being forced to rely on outsiders to achieve her own goals.

And what the Kuritans had done since...

The sound of an approaching vehicle cut off her thoughts, and she descended the snow-covered steps toward the gated entrance. Her guards straightened unconsciously in response to her demeanor, and followed her down the steps as the Morningstar command vehicle pulled into the compound, with a pair of escorting Minion hovertanks settling into cautious defensive positions on either side. While the likelihood of any threat reaching them within the HPG compound's defensive perimeter was miniscule, she respected their caution, even if the necessity disappointed her.

The Morningstar, as well as two lances of Minion hovertanks, had been loaned from Warrior House Imarra. The Morningstar was known for its command-and-control abilities, especially in an urban environment, and the Minions were fast, light hovertanks specifically designed for urban combat, heavier than the traditional Pegasus scout tanks and Tamerlane strike sleds that made up a significant percentage of her own rapid-response force.

The Minions had been specifically designed to root out stubborn resistance in cities, and she had already seen signs that they would be needed in their primary role. While the people of Northwind, specifically those who lived in the city of Tara, had once been Capellan citizens many decades before, the years under Federated Commonwealth and Republic of the Sphere rule had caused previous loyalties to wane. While there had been little active resistance to the Capellan occupation, likely due to the Confederation's history of brutal responses to insurgents, the angry glares and increasingly prolific graffiti were stark reminders that the people saw her as a conqueror, not a liberator.

The hinged door on the side of the Morningstar opened upward, and *Gao-shiao-zhang* Jiang Hui stepped out in only his uniform, seemingly unaffected by the bitter winter chill. Two House Imarra warriors in practical full weather gear took up guard positions outside the command vehicle's door.

Hui smiled warmly as he met her at the foot of the steps. "Good morning, *Sang-shao*. I hope our arrival did not wake you too early."

"Not at all, *Gao-shiao-zhang*," Lindsey replied, appreciating his ever-amused tone and decision to meet her as an equal. "I trust your travels went smoothly?"

"Exceptionally so," he replied, gesturing for her to precede him into the Morningstar, and she stepped up into the command vehicle's main area. "It appears the Republic forces were content to let us come here, at least for now. I left a small picket force behind to keep them honest, but I doubt that will do much more than delay them for the immediate future. If our projections are right, the definitive battles will be here."

"We will be ready for them, sir," Lindsey said, the elder man smiling at the conviction in her voice.

"I never doubted it," Hui replied. "I trust your inspection of the FOB went well, and that *Sang-shao* Qiao is prepared to do her part?"

Lindsey glanced over quick enough to catch the small smile the *gao-shiao-zhang* allowed himself. While she knew she could never keep her little visit to the FOB from him forever, it was wise for her to remember that, despite his laid-back demeanor, the cunning man beside her had earned his current position as the head of the Confederation's premier Warrior House, and she should never underestimate him.

She nodded carefully, but her attention was drawn to the other occupants of the Morningstar.

The first she recognized instantly: *Lien-zhang* Arnold Garzon, Warrior House Imarra's second-in-command. The Grand Master's right hand, Garzon handled the majority of operational command items when Hui was engaged in other matters. While the *lien-zhang* had always been proper and respectful to her, Lindsey could not help but get the sense that he was hesitant to recognize her as his superior. Whether that had to do with the traditional Warrior House disdain for forces outside the Warrior House Orders, or something else entirely, she did not know. Still, as long as Garzon did his job and followed her orders, she was willing to let it be.

The room's second occupant truly caught her attention, however. With a carefully trimmed moustache and coiffed hair, he stood in the shadow of the holotank that dominated the command vehicle's interior. Unlike Hui and Garzon, this man was wearing a plain black jumpsuit of military cut, but with no insignia, which meant he was not a regular military officer.

"*Sang-shao* Lindsey Baxter," Hui said by way of introduction, "this is Agent Maxwell Cheng, our Maskirovka liaison on Northwind."

Lindsey bowed her head respectfully, careful to keep her expression neutral. Like most military officers, she had a healthy respect for the work the Capellan intelligence community did for tactical planning, but she had also known far too many Mask operatives to ever say she enjoyed the experience. The *gao-shiao-zhang* had met with the undercover Maskirovka liaison when the task force first arrived on planet, but she had previously been spared dealing with Cheng in person.

"*Sang-shao* Baxter," Cheng replied, his voice a careful study in neutrality. "I have heard of much of your work here in Tara."

Lindsey chose to take that comment as a compliment, and once again silently bowed her head.

Hui gave the two of them a friendly smile. "*Sang-shao*, I wanted to take a moment to get us all together and update our tactical planning, now that our deployments are complete. Do you have any updates for us?"

Lindsey focused on the updated local map displayed in the holotank. "Yes, *Gao-shiao-zhang*. As we discussed previously, I have redeployed my forces into multiple defensive perimeters, allowing for a defense in depth should the Republic move to strike at us. The majority of the Canopian Lancers are under repair as we speak, but what units are available have been integrated into patrol routes along pre-assigned vectors, where we can best use their speed as a rapid response force."

Hui nodded. "Excellent work, *Sang-shao*. Has there been any new movement on the part of the Republic?"

"Very little, sir," Lindsey replied. "There have been the occasional probes of the city limits, and the Republic troops have proven quite adept at intercepting some of our units, pulling them away from their lances, and ambushing them. I have issued new standing orders to keep our forces concentrated within the city itself, and our warriors have been forbidden to stray from their patrols in anything less than lance strength."

"Then it sounds like we are ready to take our next steps," Hui replied. "I just spoke with *Sang-shao* Qiao on the way in, and she assured me that the staging area is complete and her own forces are ready to move. The only question is, what will be our next move? Agent Cheng?"

Cheng straightened and adjusted the display with a gesture of his hand, zooming it out to a scale to show Tara itself and the plains that separated the city from the Castle. "*Sang-shao*, the Republic forces seem content to hide away in their castle since our failed attack, refusing to meet us on the battlefield in an honorable fashion and forcing us to deal with them on another level."

Lindsey managed to keep her expression under control, despite the veiled reference to her assault on the Republic base. *Of course they wouldn't meet us on the field of battle,* she thought. *What warrior would leave a strong, defensible position unless absolutely necessary?* She glanced over at Hui when the Maskirovka operative was not looking, and he gave her the flicker of a knowing smile.

Cheng continued, either missing the shared look or being too tactful to acknowledge it. "With Laurel's Legion in place to counter any breakouts from the Castle, we believe it is time to begin extending our own hold on the region. Warrior House Imarra is prepared to begin a new siege on the Castle, ensuring that we bottle up the defenders until we can whittle down their strength and redeploy to take the citadel once and for all.

Lindsey nodded, keeping her irritation from showing. It *was* a good plan—mostly because it was the exact same one she had attempted several days ago! Admittedly, they had much better odds of success now: there was little chance of additional Republic reinforcements coming this time, and with the fresh might of House Imarra and Laurel's Legion able to respond to any attempts to circumvent the siege, the plan had an excellent chance of succeeding. "How may we assist, *Gao-shiao-zhang?*"

Hui looked at her squarely, his expression unreadable. "We believe the best thing you can do right now is convince the Draconis Combine forces to support our moves against the Republic."

She felt her expression go very still. *So he does blame me,* she thought. She had already failed to take the Castle once, so the *gao-shiao-zhang* would do it himself. She flattered herself to think that Hui respected her enough to not make such a choice without discussing it with her, so she assumed Cheng had been the driving force behind it.

Still, she was an officer in the CCAF, and there was very little else she could say. "Of course, *Gao-shiao-zhang.*"

"I know it is not ideal, Lindsey," Hui replied, using her given name to soften the blow. "I know it is the last thing I would want to do either, but it is imperative that we find out what their intentions are. Not to mention, many of your own units are still undergoing repairs from the battle at the Castle, and you remain our primary defensive force for both the HPG and the city. You have proven you can hold Tara against whatever the Republic throws at you, so I would be a fool to change something that works."

Lindsey nodded, understanding the logic even as she internally railed against it. Still, she focused on something else the elder warrior had said. "Do we have a concern that the Kuritan forces are not here to support us?"

Hui's gaze flickered to Cheng, and she saw the Maskirovka liaison's expression tighten. "Mr. Cheng seems to be of the opinion that we should not rely too much on the altruistic nature of our Unity Pact allies."

Cheng nodded, his face serious. "The timing of their arrival is highly suspect, as is their current placement in orbit. Instead of immediately landing and allowing us to jointly negate the Republic threat, they seem content to hang over our heads like the Sword of Damocles. I would demand a tangible showing of their support before I would consider relying on them."

Lindsey nodded, understanding his point while still wondering if he had more intelligence on the situation than he was revealing. Did Cheng already have reports hinting that their allies were less than reliable, or was the Maskirovka's well-known disdain for all foreign nations showing though?

Still, there was little else she could do. "I will reach out to the Kuritan forces immediately, *Gao-shiao-zhang*."

"Thank you, *Sang-shao*. Dismissed," Hui replied.

Lindsey departed with a respectful nod to the three men, but to her complete lack of surprise, Hui followed her back out into the cold.

Once they were safely out of the command vehicle, he turned to her, his expression more contrite than she would have expected. "I'm sorry, Lindsey. I know this is not the mission you wanted, but we must learn the intentions of our Kuritan visitors. If they are here to assist us, they must agree to joint tactical planning so we can make the best use of our collective resources."

She looked at him intently. "And if they are not here to assist us?"

Hui's expression hardened. "Then your mission remains the same: continue to hold the HPG against all who would seek to take it from us, and give us the time we need to push them off the planet."

Lindsey shook her head, smiling. They both knew he had recommended she send out the call for reinforcements that had brought them to this point. "I understand. Until we know what their intentions are, we cannot use our forces to the greatest extent."

"Thank you, *Sang-shao*," he replied, sounding truly grateful.

Now she looked at him squarely. "Thank me when I succeed."

CHAPTER 5

"I remember my father telling me about two of the most important questions in the galaxy, a quote from one of his favorite old vids: 'Who do you serve, and who do you trust?'"

—*Sang-shao* Lindsey Baxter, in a private message
to *Sang-shao* Julie Qiao, 7 December 3150

HPG COMPOUND
TARA, NORTHWIND
REPUBLIC OF THE SPHERE
7 DECEMBER 3150

Striding down into the main command area for the HPG's conventional communications suite, Lindsey Baxter gave her surroundings a customary once-over, ensuring that nothing behind her could compromise the image she intended to project to the Kuritan general. She knew all too well how her gender might play to the man, and wanted to ensure as few distractions as possible. While she would rather have made this call from the privacy of her own quarters—for operational security if nothing else—she though it important to talk from a position of strength, ensuring that the approaching Combine forces knew she had full control over the HPG compound. While unsure she believed Agent Cheng's concerns about the Combine's motives on Northwind, a little precaution never hurt.

Not for the first time did she regret the chain of circumstance that made her the point person for this communication. She had no doubt the *gao-shiao-zhang* would get far more instinctive respect from the Kuritan warrior, but Hui was currently overseeing preparations for renewed engagement against the Republic forces. The arrival of Countess Tara Campbell's troops had complicated the strategic picture across the planet, and the Capellan commanders had been careful to consolidate their strength, ensuring they maintained local superiority in the face of the Republic reinforcements. The faster, more advanced Republic units, coupled with the Highlanders' knowledge of the local terrain, made any sort of equal conflict between the two sides a risky process at best, and she fully agreed with the *gao-shiao-zhang*'s decision to merge their forces with the Kuritans.

Still, that didn't change the fact that she had to deal with their commander.

She glanced down at one of the technicians manning the communications console. "Put me through to the Kuritan flagship. Full holo please."

The commtech confirmed the order as his hands moved deftly across the console. Moments later the holoscreen consolidated into the three-dimensional display of the senior Kuritan officer.

Sho-sho Hisao Ikeda was every centimeter the Combine warrior, every raven-colored hair in place, and his perfect posture made his duty uniform look like formal dress. Had she not known who this man was before he reached out, she would have recognized the cold glint in his eyes anywhere.

She gave the holographic figure a measured nod. "Welcome to the Northwind system, *Sho-sho*. I am—"

"*Sang-shao* Baxter, I presume?" the Combine commander interrupted. "I am *Sho-sho* Hisao Ikeda. My Hikage and our fellow Kuritan warriors have come to render assistance to our Unity Pact allies in their time of need."

"We appreciate your presence here, *Sho-sho*," Lindsey replied, careful to keep her voice pleasant and neutral.

"How could we be anywhere else, especially after receiving such a request from our allies?"

Lindsey tried to gain a sense of whether he was being condescending, but she could not gauge his sincerity. Regardless, she reminded herself, they did need the *sho-sho*'s help, and if it was up to her to make the first impression, she would succeed.

The Chancellor required no less.

"May I ask your deployment timetable, *Sho-sho*?"

There was a long pause, and for a moment she thought they had lost the signal. She was moments away from turning to check with the staff when she saw Ikeda finally reply.

"We are currently gathering intelligence on the situation on planet," he said, his expression remaining inscrutable. "We will gladly make you aware of our deployments in time for you to rendezvous with us."

There it is. She pushed down the sharp flash of anger at the insinuation that she would be subservient to the Kuritan warrior.

"Is there any way we can assist you with your deployment planning?" she asked, ensuring that her voice did not betray her thoughts. "Our forces have been on-planet for several days, and we have current intelligence that will allow you to coordinate with our operations."

Once again, a pause, but this time it was clearly deliberate on the *sho-sho*'s part. "We appreciate your willingness to assist us, *Sang-shao*, but I believe using our own resources to verify the accuracy and timeliness of your intel is our best step at this time. If you can arrange for your Maskirovka liaison to send up your raw data immediately, I will have my staff begin processing it."

She gave Ikeda an insincere smile, her anger quickly giving way to concern. While she could not contest the *sho-sho* wanting to verify the intelligence for himself, he had clearly phrased the request to put doubt on the Capellans' own intelligence-gathering capabilities while highlighting his own experience in the area. Not to mention, while the Kuritan officer had intimated that his forces would be making a deployment to assist their Capellan allies, he had been careful not to put forth a timetable nor to commit to any particular course of action, even to the point of agreeing to a specific joint operation planning. "I will have the intelligence reports and the raw data sent up to your flagship immediately. We look forward to coordinating with you further at your convenience, *Sho-sho*."

The *sho-sho* gave a condescending smile and then cut the circuit.

Lindsey waited for a brief moment, then glanced down at her technician. "Please reach out to the *gao-shiao-zhang* and transfer our most up-to-date information to Ikeda's flagship. If the *gao-shiao-zhang* or our Kuritan friends need me, I will be on my personal comm."

She gave a final glance around the command center to ensure all was well, then headed out into the corridor at a measured pace. She took merely a moment to ensure the space was deserted and the door had closed behind her before swearing fluently in four different languages, mostly in regards to the Kuritan commander's dubious parentage and several anatomical acts that were likely impossible and, in one case, potentially fatal.

She stopped suddenly when she heard the double doors behind her open again and turned with a composed face to whomever had followed her out.

"Well, I am not quite sure he could do that," Qiao replied with a smirk. "However, I am quite sure I would like to see him try."

"Welcome back," Lindsey replied, choosing to ignore the comment. "Is everything all right at the FOB?"

"Yes. I was just moving some of my jump-capable BattleMechs to my DropShip, just in case there is an issue with the Kuritans. I think the *gao-shiao-zhang* was hoping you would divert me if there was a need."

Lindsey nodded, seeing Grand Master's point. With her holding down the fort in the city, it made sense to send Laurel's Legion back immediately, especially since they would need a command officer in the field if they needed to deploy quickly.

"Doesn't seem like there'll be any risk of that anytime soon," Lindsey replied, allowing a brief flash of irritation to show on her face. "Did you hear any of that?"

"Only the part where he tried to hedge his bets while he asked you to give him your deployment plans," Qiao replied, and Lindsey felt a wave of instinctive relief at her agreement.

"So, you also think he is trying to poach things?"

"Without a doubt," her fellow *sang-shao* replied. "I think it is exactly what we thought it might be when we heard the Kuritans had jumped into the system—they are waiting to see how they can best capitalize on the whole situation. If they think they will get the better of us all by securing the HPG station for themselves and leaving us out to dry, I have no doubt they will try to do it."

"But what about the treaty?"

Qiao shrugged. "What about it? You know as well as I that the Unity Pact has no provisions for this sort of situation. Whether Ikeda should succeed or fail, he has a multitude of options available. Governments throughout history have become expert at the task of disavowing commanders who exceeded their authority, and the Coordinator is pragmatic to a fault. Even if our 'allies' try take the HPG from us and fail, they will still be able to claim it was all just a big misunderstanding." She glanced at Lindsey. "I am assuming that is the reason both of you were recording the conversation."

"Of course. Standard procedure."

"So, since we do not know what our ally is going to do, but we do know he is not going to act quickly, it looks like we continue on without them. The trick now is to make sure we cover all our bases and use our alliance to the best of our ability...without showing the Kuritans our backs."

"Agreed," Lindsey replied. "Any news from the front?"

"At the moment, the Republic can't know our situation with the Kuritans. They know there's an enemy force hanging above their heads, and it could come down nearly anywhere. They need to defend the whole planet, while we have a much narrower scope of what we need to protect."

Qiao was right, and Lindsey had already considered the same points. "The problem is what they might do with that knowledge. If the Republic suspects the Kuritans' presence will give us the tactical flexibility we currently lack, what would they be tempted to do?"

Qiao's eyes lit up with an epiphany. "They'll want to fight us on ground that cannot be easily or quickly reinforced."

"Which means there's an excellent chance they're going to make a bid for Tara," Lindsey confirmed. "Trying to combat-drop into a city would be a stone bitch, and any landing they make outside the city would be slow and time consuming. As long as our Kuritan friends continue to hang out up there in orbit, it is only a matter of time before someone on the Republic side gets a bright idea to make a play for the HPG compound."

Not to mention, neither woman had to remind herself that Northwind was just a single planet on the vast galactic stage. With uncontested control of the HPG, the Capellan Confederation could wreak havoc on this entire front of the Republic theater, but with them trying to fight for their lives on a daily basis, there was little time for data collection and collation that didn't have to do with their current and more immediate problem. Lindsey had been trying to conscript additional research assets in the hopes of having a greater effect on the war, but had been mostly unsuccessful. The ComStar staff had evaded capture during the initial seizure of the HPG compound and slipped into the city's shadows, and she had no doubt that many of them had gone to the Highlanders for protection.

Glancing over at her friend, Lindsey gave her a thin smile. "Well, I have done my duty... Now I feel like going to find a good, stiff drink. You in?"

"Always," Qiao replied, and the two women continued on down the hallway.

UNION-CLASS DROPSHIP *BLISTERING WIND*
GEOSYNCHRONOUS ORBIT
NORTHWIND
REPUBLIC OF THE SPHERE
7 DECEMBER 3150

Sho-sho Hisao Ikeda stepped away from the bridge of his DropShip, his magnetized boots slowing his usually swift gait. He glanced over at his aide, *Chu-sa* Ivan Hallow, with a curious expression on his face. "What do you think, Ivan?"

For a long moment, his adjutant remained silent, but not through any sense of concern. The two men had worked together for a long time, and Ikeda had come to rely on the cautious, steady approach of one of his closest advisors. The *sho-sho* waited patiently, a gift he would give to very few people in his life.

"I believe you are right to be concerned, *Sho-sho*," Hallow said. "It sounds like the *sang-shao* is acutely aware of how thinly they have stretched themselves to make this bid for the HPG facility, and with the arrival of additional Republic forces, they are concerned about their ability to hold the city."

"What do you think their chances are?"

This time, Ikeda did not need to wait for his aide's response. "I think they forget that the HPG is in the heart of Tara, and Tara is the heart of Northwind. While the homesteads and smaller cities will always have a rough charm, due to the clannish nature of the planet, nearly every one of them has family, friends, or those they love in the city. They will not allow it to stay in enemy hands for long, no matter what the Capellans say. I fear that these...Capellan mercenaries will have underestimated that fact."

Ikeda allowed himself a small nod, instead of correcting his aide. While Hallow knew McCarron's Armored Cavalry and Laurel's Legion were CCAF units, and had technically left their mercenary past behind nearly a century ago, he could not seem to let their previous allegiance pass without comment.

"We need to remember that these 'mercenaries' are not the only ones in play, however," Ikeda reminded his subordinate. "They are commanded by the Grand Master of their Warrior Houses, and I doubt this Jiang Hui is a man who shies away from the requirements of necessity. What do you think of that?"

"I think our best method is to convince the *gao-shiao-zhang* that decisive action is the requirement of the day," Hallow replied.

"You want to have the Capellans do the dirty work for us?"

"We will be doing the Coordinator no favors by putting the blood of innocents on our own hands, *Sho-sho*. However, the Capellan Chancellor is a pragmatic man, and his family has shown that they know the requirements of their position. I have little doubt that his Warrior House members know their duties just as well."

Ikeda nodded, seeing exactly where his aide was going, applauding the Machiavellian nature of his planning. If the Capellans did strike at the people of Tara, the Highlanders would be honor-bound to respond, which would force them onto a battlefield not of their own choosing. Split by circumstances and sandwiched between the Capellans and the Kuritan forces, they would quickly see defeat in detail, and the planet would belong to the Combine.

Fortunately, if the two sides did not go for the plan, his forces had the freedom to continue watching from where they were, allowing the Republic and the Capellans to beat themselves bloody before dealing with either side.

Not to mention, Ikeda thought, *the odds are good that my own reinforcements would arrive before any of theirs.* With an extra DCMS regiment or two, he could take on all comers, ensuring that neither side could capitalize on the threat.

And if they could just take care of those JumpShips...

He pulled away from the seductive thoughts of repaying his allies in kind, allowing his gaze to slip back to the starscape slowly shifting on his wall viewer.

CHAPTER 6

"Darryl, I hate to do this to you while you are on your way back, but I need you and Scott to run downtown to meet with Lyle and Bill. Seamus thinks he lost something, but he doesn't have time to go back and find it. Since ye owe me one, I told him we would help out..."

—Coded message from Cathy Glazier to Darryl Huss,
8 December 3150

HPG COMPOUND
TARA, NORTHWIND
REPUBLIC OF THE SPHERE
8 DECEMBER 3150

Julie Qiao's image from the cockpit of her *Emperor* was projected on the small screen on Lindsey Baxter's desk, and what little of her face was visible through her neurohelmet visor showed her own thoughtfulness. "What do you think it means?" she said, in response to Lindsey recounting her conversation with Ikeda.

For a brief moment, Lindsey felt guilty for contacting her fellow commander before she returned to the FOB, but her conversation with the Hikage leader yesterday continued to vex her. She knew her gender might be an issue due to the Draconis Combine's misogynistic views of women as the weaker sex, but she would have thought her position as a commander of one of the most impressive military units in the Inner Sphere would have bought her a certain amount of respect.

Or was it McCarron's Armored Cavalry's mercenary past that rankled the *sho-sho* so much? The Draconis Combine had a dark history with warriors who sold their services, going back to the Wolf's Dragoons incident in the 3020s and Takashi Kurita's subsequent Death to Mercenaries order, but surely a modern commander would be able to get past that!

She shook her head, clearing the thought and concentrating back on Qiao. "I don't know if it means anything yet. What I do know is that every moment that we wait, we allow the Republic forces to rearm and resupply, and we let them have the initiative. If we don't do something soon..."

Qiao nodded. "What does the *gao-shiao-zhang* have to say?"

For the briefest of moments, Lindsey was tempted to come clean, but she managed to keep her composure. The last thing Qiao needed for her self-esteem was to know the deal she had cut with the *gao-shiao-zhang*, and Lindsey hoped she would never have to reveal it to Qiao, who was rapidly becoming a trusted friend. "He allowed me to take the lead on our negotiations. I offered to let him take over, thinking he might make the Combine forces a little more willing to listen, but he thinks it best we maintain a single point of contact. The *gao-shiao-zhang* has been rallying our forces, preparing the main strike when it comes."

"He's probably right, you know," Qiao said, surprising her for a moment. "At least about the Kuritans."

"What do you mean?" Lindsey asked curiously.

"It's plausible deniability. Right now, the negotiations are important but not vital to our survival. When the *gao-shiao-zhang* calls in the need for forces under the Unity Pact, the Combine commander must either accede to his request immediately or deny it, which would prove they have other things than our well-being at heart. As long as you are maintaining negotiations, it allows everyone to save face and keep everything to a slow boil—two important points that will be very important to the Combine."

Lindsey nodded, understanding the perverse sense of it. *Could this really have nothing to do with me at all? Is Ikeda just keeping his options open?*

On the screen, Qiao's head shot up, reacting to something off camera, but the instant tension in her expression told Lindsey that something had just gone terribly wrong.

"Contact! Multiple contacts on my scope!" Qiao's eyes locked with hers for a moment, and then she cut the visual feed.

Lindsey understood the situation instinctively and rose to head out of her office as quickly as she could while still remaining dignified. As she entered the main control room, she was pleased to see her command staff reacting to the same news, having received it at roughly the same time. "Sitrep."

"*Sang-shao* Qiao reports contact with multiple enemy units near the intersection of Calder and Forstchien," one of her MechWarriors, a wiry young officer named Newsom, reported. Lindsey had briefly reassigned him to her support staff due to heavy damage to his BattleMech at the Castle. "Enemy force is confirmed as a lance in strength, with light armor support. It appears to be the Grey Watch."

Lindsey nodded, not sure if she was relieved at the small unit size or more concerned about her friend facing off with such experienced warriors, despite the age of their tech. "Was this an ambush?"

"I don't think so," Cheng said from beside Lindsey, startling her with how he'd entered the command center without her noticing. "From the tonnage they are facing, it would have been an incredibly unwise gamble on the Highlanders' part, especially against a lance of that strength. She probably just stumbled a little too close to one of their holes, and they are coming to protect it like bees defending their hive."

While she knew better than to make such an assumption, having seen numerically inferior forces best more numerous and well-armed foes with the benefit of surprise and sound tactics, she conceded that Cheng's analysis was probably correct. Now that they were receiving data from Qiao's command lance, they knew the Grey Watch ambushers were primarily medium and heavy 'Mechs: not a foe to be ignored by any means, but at a significant tonnage and technology disadvantage when considering the size and strength of Qiao's lance. If they had been waiting in ambush for her unit, they likely would have either brought additional forces or chosen a more ideal place to spring their ambush.

No, Lindsey thought, *they were probably out searching for the FOB, and stumbled on Julie on her way back.*

Without prompting, the staff put feeds from the battle onto the wall screens. The main screen held a top-down view of the area, images from one of the spy satellites they had put into orbit, while the smaller screens around it showed up-to-date information on her forces, as well as computer simulations and assumptions about the attackers. She recognized a Grey Watch *Warhammer*, a *Hunchback*, a *Phoenix Hawk*, and a *Trebuchet*. As she watched, the *Trebuchet* sent a flight of missiles arcing toward Qiao's *Emperor*, and Lindsey felt her hands tighten into fists as the wave of missiles struck across the torso of her friend's 'Mech.

Never one to let such an insult go unpunished, Qiao fired back with a pair of ruby lasers, cutting away at part of the armor on the *Trebuchet*'s right arm and left leg. If the commander of Laurel's Legion had felt any initial surprise at the suddenness of the attack, it had long since dissipated, and the rest of her lance pulled tightly toward her with practiced precision, ready to provide support.

A *Men Shen* from Qiao's lance cut in front of her, trying to give her some space to maneuver, but the Grey Watch *Hunchback* reached out with its heavy autocannon, and cut one of the 'Mech's arms away in a single burst. The loss of the arm, coupled with major damage elsewhere, was enough to shift the smaller 'Mech's balance and send it toppling to the ground. While the *Men Shen* wasn't down for good, one of its lancemates moved to cover it, and fired a hasty pair of medium lasers that struck a glancing blow on the *Hunchback*'s arm.

"What's the closest support in range?" Lindsey asked Newsom.

To his credit, the young officer did not need to check his screen before responding. "We are diverting a light patrol now, and a pursuit lance from the FOB is en route. ETA, eight minutes."

"They may be dead in eight minutes! We don't have anything closer?"

"No ma'am," Newsom replied, sound abashed. "A larger force might have been spotted."

Lindsey narrowed her eyes, and somehow managed to avoid looking at Agent Cheng. While she had approved the general patrol planning for the city's interior, she had left the specifics in the hands of her staff. She could not fault Newsom for attempting to maximize his patrol coverage, but she had s sneaking suspicion Cheng had whispered such a suggestion in the young officer's ear. Glancing at him, she found the agent watching her steadily, clearly considering if she would openly accuse him for this tactical blunder.

Lindsey suppressed her initial response, instead focusing on the immediate tactical situation. When the *gao-shiao-zhang* returned, she would have a longer discussion about the Mask agent.

As if summoned, one of her comm techs spoke up. "Priority broadcast from Imarra actual. Patching through now..."

"*Sang-shao* Qiao, this is Imarra actual." Even through the communication static, Lindsey recognized Hui's voice. "We are two minutes out from your position. Prepare for counterstrike."

Lindsey reached over and quickly typed information into her console to get the direct feed from the *gao-shiao-zhang*'s *Yu Huang*, conscious of Cheng still hovering behind her. Her lips tightened into a grim line as she confirmed what she had known: Hui's command lance was en route, without waiting for the rest of his company. As a point of personal preference, the *gao-shiao-zhang* had equipped his personal lance with a set of jump-capable assault 'Mechs, hardware that could keep up with his own movement profile. She blithely remembered an earlier staff meeting, where Hui had joked that he had only accepted the mission to Northwind to get a *Highlander* to round out his lance.

A quick glance at the lay of the area also confirmed that things would be close: while the sheer mass of tonnage the *gao-shiao-zhang* had brought would be decisive in the battle, the experienced Grey Watch warriors had already found their target. The single-minded way they were focusing on Qiao's lance indicated that they knew they had one of the expedition commanders in their sights, and taking her out of the equation would have a negative effect on her regiment.

However, Hui was determined to break that equation. From Qiao's visual feed, Lindsey watched Hui's *Yu Huang* descend on twin jets of ice-blue plasma, his PPC flashing out with deadly accuracy as he landed, flaying armor from one of the *Hunchback*'s legs. In a display of exceptional marksmanship, he fired his autocannon at a different target and cut deeply into the *Trebuchet*'s chest. The autocannon fire blasted through armor as if it was not there, chewing deeply into the torso, and triggered an explosion in one of the *Trebuchet*'s ammunition bays. Long-range missiles exploded, and for a moment fire wreathed the entire top half of the BattleMech. A single glance was enough to confirm the Grey Watch 'Mech was gone.

The *Yu Huang* was focusing on the *Hunchback* when a primal roar filled the room.

It took a moment, but Lindsey eventually realized the sound had come over the Grey Watch lance's open channel, and she watched them all switch their fire to the newcomer.

The roar had to have come from the *Warhammer*. The Grey Watch warrior moved forward implacably, firing each of their weapons as quickly as they would cycle, heedless of the heat buildup that undoubtedly roasted them in their command couch. A single glance was enough to confirm that the *Warhammer* was a -6R variant, lacking the double-capacity heat sinks used by newer models. Short-range missiles and machine gun fire pitted the armor of the immense *Yu Huang*, as PPC lightning and directed energy from the medium lasers carved off whole sheets of armor from the once-pristine 'Mech.

Lindsey watched helplessly as Qiao attempted to assist Hui, but she found herself in the same place as the approaching House Imarra 'Mechs: the *Warhammer* had closed to knife-fighting range with the Capellan BattleMech, and in the tight confines of the city, a stray shot could result in friendly fire. Her hands balled into fists as she willed the other 'Mechs to hurry, or for the *Warhammer* to finally succumb to its heat.

The end came suddenly. The *Warhammer* lit off both PPCs in a final gesture of defiance as the *Yu Huang*'s autocannon cut through the center of the *Warhammer*'s chest, piercing all the way through the heat shields that protected the 'Mech's fusion heart. The added heat quickly overwhelmed the pilot, and the whole BattleMech slumped over like a marionette whose strings had been cut.

The *Warhammer* would not be denied its revenge, however. One PPC flashed over the *Yu Huang*'s shoulder, but the second one took the 90-ton assault 'Mech directly in the head. The energy glowed brightly as it lanced into the cockpit, and Lindsey stifled a yelp as the *Yu Huang* froze in place, no longer under control.

To her horror, she watched the Grand Master's 'Mech fall forward, tipping over onto its killer, and both 'Mechs crashed to the ground.

CHAPTER 7

"Reports from Tara General Hospital claim the Grand Master of Warrior House Imarra is in critical condition following the most recent of several Republic strikes on Capellan forces. All eyes are now on the Capellans, wondering what our subjugators will do next..."

—Tegan Shea, *Northwind Today*, 8 December 3150

KOHLER SPACEPORT
TARA, NORTHWIND
REPUBLIC OF THE SPHERE
8 DECEMBER 3150

Lien-zhang Arnold Garzon rushed into the Morningstar command vehicle, his face grim, having just come from the infirmary where *Gao-shiao-zhang* Hui had been admitted. Garzon had believed his commanding officer had been killed when he saw the *Yu Huang* sustain the PPC strike to the head, but while the shot had shattered the cockpit and left the *gao-shiao-zhang* in critical condition, he was still alive, and the Warrior House physicians were among the best in the CCAF. Garzon had stayed only long enough to see that his mentor was still breathing before returning to the command center, ready to seek retribution on those who had nearly cost him his commander.

The *gao-shiao-zhang*'s aim had been successful, however: while the rest of the Grey Watch lance had been driven off, *Sang-shao* Qiao had survived, and her troops were preparing to sweep through the city to find any remaining Grey Watch forces, no matter where they might hide.

Garzon was unsurprised to see the Maskirovka liaison, Agent Cheng, waiting for him.

"*Lien-zhang* Garzon, how is the Grand Master?" Cheng asked. If there was any insincerity in his voice, it was well hidden.

"He is in critical condition, but the doctors are hopeful," Garzon replied. "We should know more in a few hours."

"Excellent," Cheng said. "And are you ready to take over for the *gao-shiao-zhang*?"

Garzon clasped his hands behind his back, using the gesture to take a moment to consider his answer. "*Sang-shao* Qiao has already prepared a search grid throughout the city, and we will find the remains of this Highlanders force and deal with them."

Cheng looked at him carefully. "And what are you prepared to do, *Shiao-zhang*?

"*Shiao-zhang*? What do you mean?" Garzon asked, confused.

"With *Gao-shiao-zhang* Hui's injuries rendering him incapable of command, *you* are the acting House Master of Warrior House Imarra. As such, you are able to take the decisive steps necessary to deal with the Republic threat once and for all."

Garzon straightened, his expression a mix of concern and curiosity. "What exactly are you suggesting?"

"I am suggesting we finally move off of the defensive!" Cheng replied, showing more passion than Garzon ever remembered seeing during any of their dinners over the last several weeks. "The Republic troops have been making fools of us, hiding in their dens and then striking from ambush like the cowards they are. They have mistaken that moderation for foolishness, and now it very possibly cost the life of your Grand Master. The time has finally come for us to correct their folly."

Garzon hesitated, uncomfortable with the stirrings the words brought up in his chest. "I don't believe the *gao-shiao-zhang*—"

"With all due respect, Arnold, we have seen what Hui's restraint has brought us!" the Maskirovka operative replied harshly, his eyes locked on Garzon's. "Your focus on your leader's aims are commendable, but we need to take action! Look at what his hesitancy has wrought. The Kuritans have come to steal our prize, and hang above us like the Sword of Damocles. The *gao-shiao-zhang* has allowed two former mercenaries—and yes, no matter their length of service, that is what they are—to lead our attacks against the Republic, and these two women have achieved nothing for us."

From Cheng's expression, it was clear that no matter how much Garzon protested, and how much he tried to remind the Maskirovka operative that the strikes led by his fellow commanders had taken both Tara and the HPG compound, the Maskirovka agent was uninterested in listening. Unfortunately, that put Garzon in a very difficult position. While Cheng was not in the CCAF chain of command, ignoring his counsel could be a dangerous proposition, especially if it could later be seen as compromising the goals of the Confederation.

"What do you propose?" Garzon asked.

"The same thing I proposed in the first place. We currently hold the city, and we hold more of it than we need. I recommend we begin razing it to the ground, block by fetid block, and allow our forces to take the best defensive positions from the rubble."

"You would have us attack civilians?"

"I would have us threaten civilians in the residential sector," Cheng replied, giving a sly smile. "You can see from the intelligence I provided that we believe some of these Grey Watch units have been spotted in the city, sheltered by the citizens of Tara. The Grand Master had been careful to avoid the residential sector to prevent triggering a larger conflict, but I believe now is exactly the time to strike. Whether we actually threaten the citizens of Tara is incidental: if the Grey Watch sees House Imarra moving in force toward the residential sector, they will respond."

Garzon stared down at the holographic display before him, seeking a moment to think. While the thought would normally be horrifying, he remembered looking down at the gaunt, bandaged face of Jiang Hui, and wondered if his methods had brought them to this point.

Could Cheng be right? Garzon thought. *We have been showing restraint due to the* gao-shiao-zhang's *wishes, but the people of Northwind have not bent the knee as they should have. It is only natural for them to want to fight back, but as former Confederation citizens, they should know their rightful place.*

"If we begin attacking," Cheng continued, "the Republic forces might continue to cower in their redoubt, but the Highlanders and Grey Watch certainly will not. This is their home after all, and they will never allow us to defile it, as we would never allow them to defile Sian. The Republic, however, has no such backbone, nor will they take a stand for their own mercenary kin... No, this will be the wedge we need to keep them from working together, and potentially allow us to strike at them before the Kuritans lose patience and take advantage of our own disorganization."

Cheng softened his voice into a more reasonable tone. "Yes, the Kuritans. If they are as treacherous as we both believe, they will surely strike at us the moment an opportunity appears. If they drop troops on top of us, either during or after our attack on the entrenched Republic forces, we will not be able to disengage in time to protect the city. No matter how skilled we are, we don't have the means to fight both of them!"

As the Maskirovka agent walked slowly around the holotable, there was something vicious in his expression. "However, you can leave the Kuritans to me. I know exactly what must be done, and I have already taken steps to ensure they will not be a problem. What we need, however, is the Highlanders and Republic forces neutralized, and quickly. The only question is, are we up to the task?"

For a long moment, Garzon considered everything Cheng had said, and just as important, what he had not said—namely that, as a Maskirovka agent outside the CCAF's chain of command, Cheng could not order a Capellan officer to take a specific action, but he could strongly suggest it. While Cheng had phrased it as if it was the two of them against the enemy, Garzon knew that, as Imarra's acting *shiao-zhang*, the final decision had to be his.

Traditionally, the question of priorities would never even pass through his mind. Like all members of Warrior House Imarra, he recognized the tenets of the Lorix Creed above all others, which focused on loyalty to the Warrior House and the Chancellor. However, the question was whether adherence to the goals of the *gao-shiao-zhang*—and by extension, House Imarra—conflicted with the goals of the Chancellor and the Confederation.

In the end, there was no choice, as the creed was clear: *The highest and most important ideal in any MechWarrior's life is loyalty: to the citizenry they protect, to the state that provides, and to the chief executive of the state, who is the MechWarrior's commander-in-chief.*

After a long moment, Garzon nodded, finding the resolution within himself as he remembered looking down at the still form of the *gao-shiao-zhang*. His expression hardened as he remembered how vibrant Hui had been in life, but now was desperately fighting for his life in the surgical bay.

"I can do it," he said.

This time, there could be no doubt: the Maskirovka agent's expression was positively predatory. "Then we shall."

HPG COMPOUND
TARA, NORTHWIND
REPUBLIC OF THE SPHERE
8 DECEMBER 3150

Lindsey Baxter walked the catwalks below the HPG's parabolic dish, showing just enough care to avoid falling, but heedless of either the icy breeze or the potential for the metal superstructure to freeze. She had forced herself to come up here to avoid pacing in the communications center itself, knowing others had tuned into her growing frustration.

It wasn't just how she was being treated by their supposed allies from the Draconis Combine; she was beginning to feel more and more isolated as the days went on. Julie Qiao had returned to FOB Romeo to command their forward forces. With the Canopians nearly wiped out despite all their work to build back up to combat readiness, Laurel's Legion was left as the primary offensive force capable of threatening the Republic troops at the Castle.

It did not help that her other primary offensive unit, Warrior House Imarra, had become less communicative since the wounding of *Gao-shiao-zhang* Hui. While they were not going so far as to be insubordinate, Baxter was attempting to tread carefully on the Warrior Houses' traditional autonomy, knowing that Garzon, now as acting *shiao-zhang* of Imarra, technically held equal rank. In their brief conversations, he had been curt to the point of brusqueness, and Lindsey was getting the distinct feeling that he blamed her for his master's injuries.

With Hui wounded, Qiao at the front, and Centrella-Tompkins attempting to recover from her losses, Lindsey was finding herself isolated to the point of frustration. The last thing she wanted was to let any of her subordinates to see her in this state, or worse, for the Kuritans to take it as a further sign of weakness to justify their actions.

"*Sang-shao?*"

The soft voice caused Lindsey's step to hitch for a moment, and she grabbed one of the handrails as she turned. Behind her, at a respectful, nonthreatening distance, stood Adept Bianca Haller, the young ComStar technician, waiting patiently to be recognized. From the light dusting of snow on her ebony coat, she had clearly been out here for several moments before announcing herself. In the distance, Lindsey saw one of her infantrymen watching, out of earshot, but close enough where he could use the pistol on his hip should the ComStar technician be any sort of threat to his commanding officer.

Lindsey pasted a welcoming smile on her face for the young woman, hoping Bianca had not noticed the momentary lapse. While at first she had been concerned about the loyalties of the ComStar staff she relied on to run the HPG center, she had quickly found the technicians a respectful, apolitical lot. ComStar may have been one of the first groups to reach out and take Exarch Devlin Stone's vision of peace at face value, but this particular group held onto the treasured neutrality ComStar had once provided, not seeking to involve themselves into the power plays of Northwind, but content to maintain their research and help send out HPG messages as instructed.

The arrangement had worked out so well that Lindsey had found herself warming to Bianca, less as a friend than a respected coworker. The younger woman seemed a little too fashion-conscious for Lindsey's taste, but whenever she saw Bianca, she remembered a secondary-school friend who had strummed similar emotional chords in her younger years, back when they had been inseparable.

Lindsey smiled again, making sure that Bianca saw it. "Yes?"

"Mr. Cheng has been looking for you, ma'am."

Lindsey's lips thinned in distaste, and didn't bother to hide it. It was hardly a state secret how she felt about the Maskirovka agent, and Bianca had proven perceptive enough to know the two Capellans were not the closest of coworkers. "Thank you, Ms. Haller. I will be down presently."

Bianca nodded and then turned back to depart.

Suddenly, however, Lindsey found herself less eager to be alone. "Adept Haller..."

If Bianca seemed surprised, she did not show it. "*Sang-shao*?"

"Are you...upset that we are here?"

Bianca calmly assessed the question for a moment, not necessarily out of fear for her own life, but seemingly to give it the consideration it deserved. "That is a hard question to answer, ma'am. Our research has been disrupted by the...change in management...and I miss those who lost their lives during the takeover. However, I am not so naive as to think this is any different than what has happened many times before on Northwind, the way of governments and wars." She shrugged slightly. "You had your objectives and completed them to the best of your ability. I don't like that it came to pass, but I can't blame you for it."

"True, but our focus should always be on limiting war to strictly military targets."

"We all do what we must," Bianca replied. "It hasn't slipped anyone's notice that you used a far more restrained touch than we were told to expect from an occupying Capellan force."

This time, Lindsey did smile thinly. "You will find that not all of us are the villains the rest of the Inner Sphere makes us out to be."

Bianca shrugged more expressively this time, shifting her blond locks over her shoulder. "I don't think anyone really sets out to be the villain in their own story, except in bad fiction. As I said, you have your objectives, and I appreciate that you have gone to such lengths to make completing those objectives as bloodlessly as possible for the people of Northwind."

"I try," Lindsey said, her own thoughts growing cold and brittle. "However, how can I justify that when my objectives are clear?"

"I think you must do what you think is right, *Sang-shao*," Bianca answered, bowing her head a bit. "I won't say that I am happy to hear you mention the possibility. I have been posted on Northwind for a while now, and several of the people you are fighting I consider my friends...but I also know that you are one of the reasons things have not boiled over."

"Oh?" Lindsey raised her chin, curious at the response. "What do you mean?"

"You know the Highlanders' history, ma'am. They take the protection of their home personally. It's one of the reasons they have fought you so hard. However, you have maintained the Ares Conventions, and they have respected that. You have both fought as cleanly as possible, and while war will never be bloodless, it is certainly all we could have hoped for."

For a moment, Lindsey wondered if Bianca had heard what Cheng had recommended, or whether she had come to this conclusion on her own. They had been very careful to keep their conversations private, but this ComStar scientist had a keen mind, and Lindsey didn't put it past her to have figured it out on her own.

She turned back toward the view of the city, watching the snow fall softly like a gentle carpet of white that stretched endless out to the horizon. "Sometimes it is difficult to allow for all of the variables in a situation."

"Especially when they keep compounding exponentially," Bianca replied, and Lindsey nodded. Bianca knew what she was talking about: with the Draconis Combine forces now in play, there was a great chance things were going to go in a very different direction, and quickly.

"I assume you heard the message from the Hikage commander?"

"Yes, ma'am. It is a small facility."

"And what do you think?"

If Bianca was surprised to be asked her opinion, she didn't show it. "I think he is trying to cover all his bases. Like you, he has a variety of responsibilities, but a very different perspective on the situation." Lindsey gestured for her to continue, but Bianca hesitated. "I don't mean to speak out of turn..."

"No, I am curious as to your thoughts. Please."

"Well, regardless of your goals or alliance, you are the one who first landed on this planet. You have fought the Republic, and you have taken control of this compound. That is something your Draconis Combine counterpart has not accomplished. It allows him a greater deal of...flexibility in his response."

Lindsey nodded, having had the same thoughts as well. Without the necessity of needing to fight off the Republic, the Combine forces could watch and wait for a victor. As long as matters stayed quiet for the immediate future, the reprieve would give them a greater chance to strike later. "So, you think they are waiting for an opportunity?"

"I am a scientist who believes in homeostasis," Bianca replied. "For now, everything has momentarily held to a certain sort of balance. But everything is potentially at risk to be acted on by an outside force."

"Everything can be affected by outside forces," Lindsey replied. "The real question is whether it be for good or for ill."

"That is for better minds than mine to figure out, ma'am," Bianca said, returning to a semblance of formality. "I just hope we never have to find out."

CHAPTER 8

"Colonel, it's all going to hell over here! We are showing massive Capellan movements toward the residential quarter. We are in desperate need of assistance!"

—Message from Cathy Glazier to Colonel Michael Griffin,
9 December 3150

THE CASTLE
NORTHWIND
REPUBLIC OF THE SPHERE
9 DECEMBER 3150

Declan Casey ran toward the sound of the klaxons wailing throughout the 'Mech bay, and found Lady Maeve Stirling at the foot of her *Tundra Wolf 3*. She was directing her warriors to mount up with practiced precision, despite the chaotic mass of people running through the room.

"What's going on?" he asked as she nodded at him.

The Knight's voice was taut with tension. "The Capellans have gone crazy. From what we have heard, we brought down one of their commanders when they stumbled on a Grey Watch patrol, and they're moving to take it out on civilians in the city. The Grey Watch forces inside the city are trying to hold them back, but they are simply outnumbered. I'm taking some of my troops to assist."

"What about the Hastati? I didn't get a call—"

"You unit's on standby, preparing for a counterattack by Laurel's Legion. Legion BattleMechs are already en route, and we have to treat it as a real attack, even though it is probably just a feint to keep us from reinforcing the Grey Watch."

Declan nodded, understanding completely. By feigning a strike at the Castle, the Capellans forced the Republic to make a terrible choice: defend their final redoubt or assist the Grey Watch in the city. Declan did not doubt for a moment what the Grey Watch's decision would be, and he knew they would fight to the last before seeing the people of Tara suffer.

His thoughts were disrupted by a group of MechWarriors outside the senior tech's office, gathered around one of the screens that had been turned to the local news. Declan was not sure how the broadcast had gotten through the Capellans' jamming, but the footage engrossed him as someone pumped up the volume. On the screen, a familiar news anchor stared grimly at the camera, her fists clenched on the desktop before her.

"This is Tegan Shea from *Northwind Today* with a breaking story. We are getting reports that Warrior House Imarra is systematically destroying buildings throughout midtown, apparently in retribution for a recent ambush that critically wounded their leader, Grand Master Jiang Hui. We take you now to live footage..."

A collective gasp went up from the assorted soldiers as the first scenes of destruction played out on the display. Although the footage was shot from midtown, which had been mostly cleared of inhabitants, panicked civilians ran in every direction before the unstoppable Capellan juggernaut. A quick cut showed a small corner deli Declan remembered going to with his late brother James, and he watched in horror as a House Imarra *Jinggau* leveled it with a single kick, as a man he recognized as the owner fled from the collapsing structure.

Something hard solidified in Declan's chest at the sight, and he turned to Maeve as others ran to their own BattleMechs. "How can I help?"

She looked at him oddly. "Aren't you on duty?"

"My *Marauder II* is still in repairs, so I am temporarily without a 'Mech," he replied, fighting through the instinctive pain the admission caused him.

Maeve nodded in sympathy, and then looked at him oddly. "Have you ever piloted anything lighter than an assault 'Mech for any length of time?"

Declan nodded, understanding her purpose behind the question. While, in theory, a MechWarrior should be able to pilot any BattleMech, warriors occasionally focused on what they knew. Luckily, Declan had been raised in a family that believed in being prepared for a large number of possibilities. "I learned on my granddad's *Marauder*, and I piloted a *Phoenix Hawk* in basic. If you've got it, I can pilot it."

She smirked. "I might have something for you then." Her gaze slid down the row of BattleMechs, and he followed her gaze to a single dark gantry, with a barely visible 'Mech still within.

Declan found himself breathing carefully, a strange feeling of peace within him despite the threat to the city. While the darkness obscured most of the outline of the birdlike BattleMech within, he easily recognized the *Osprey* that had carried a friend and lancemate into her final battle.

"I'm in."

Having updated the *Osprey* to his neural specifications thanks to the heroic work of the chief tech and his team, Declan was able to move out in record time. The unfamiliar birdlike gait took a moment to get used to, but he found he enjoyed the medium 'Mech's fleet, low profile.

It also felt very right to be piloting this particular 'Mech to go to the rescue of the people of Tara and the Grey Watch. His lancemate Ellie Taggart had died in this very *Osprey*, but it had also been one of the first 'Mechs repaired in the wake of the battle at the Castle, as much an honor to its fallen MechWarrior as to get it back into service. Unfortunately, in the wake of the battle the Hastati had more 'Mechs than pilots, and the *Osprey* had waited until this moment to serve again. For a brief moment he wondered if General McNamara had reserved it specifically for such a contingency.

Maeve's lance had already headed out at full throttle, but Declan's nimble little 'Mech was more than capable of catching up with them.

"Nice of you to join us, Lieutenant," she said over the main channel. "I hope you had enough time for a nap."

Declan grinned, but the expression faded as they approached Tara, where fires were visible in the distance. Black, oily smoke curled upward to blanket the city.

"Heads up, people. We have incoming."

The Capellan forces had anticipated their arrival. Several BattleMechs, their insignias marking them as the remains of the Canopian force that had been shattered at the NMA, milled about the outskirts of the city, having seen the approach of Maeve's lance. Two enemy lances sprinted toward them, attempting to close the distance quickly.

Unfortunately for them, the Knight's command lance had been configured for both speed and flexibility. Maeve fired her *Tundra Wolf*'s PPCs, and her other 'Mechs loosed long-range weapons at their opponents, causing damage even from extreme range.

Declan also fired his own weapons. His multi-missile launcher peppered an *Anubis* with long-range missiles, and then his Gauss rifle ripped the light 'Mech's right arm clean off.

The Canopian 'Mechs fared even worse as Maeve's lance maintained full speed to close the distance. While they moved into range of the smaller 'Mechs, receiving damage themselves, the sheer weight of the lance's firepower quickly cut the legs out from two of the approaching Canopians, and took a third down with a cored fusion engine.

"Don't slow down!" the Knight commanded. "We have another lance in our wake, and they'll clean up after us. We don't stop until we reach the Grey Watch."

A chorus of affirmatives came over the command channel as the Republic MechWarriors plunged down their respective streets, homing in on the last signals from the Grey Watch 'Mechs. The signals were unnecessary. The lance just needed to follow the sound of autocannon fire and the shimmering flicker of flames.

Turning a corner sharply, Declan found himself facing the back of an Imarra *Thunder* that had cornered a familiar Grey Watch *Hunchback* whose tartan told him it was piloted by Darryl Huss. The two BattleMechs were dueling with their heavy autocannons, but the larger Capellan BattleMech had a lot more armor to lose.

Taking advantage of the Capellan's distraction, Declan triggered his Gauss rifle and followed up with his extended-range medium lasers and a brace of short-range missiles. The Gauss slug and lasers pierced the *Thunder*'s vulnerable rear torso, and the missiles stabbed right through the gaps in the armor. A chain of small explosions tore at the 'Mech's internals, the damage forcing it to retreat behind a nearby building.

"Thanks for the assist!" said a familiar voice, and Declan triggered his comms.

"You're welcome, Darryl!"

"Dec! You've gotten shorter since I saw you last," Darryl replied as he lit off his medium lasers at a target Declan couldn't see. "Did you come for that drink you owe me?"

"I heard you needed help, so I took the first ride I had." Declan focused on a new target, a pristine *Sha Yu* whose stealth armor blurred its profile on his sensors.

The Imarra warrior discharged its full complement of lasers at Declan's BattleMech. One of the large lasers missed, cutting into the stone wall beside him, but the other one stabbed into the armor over his left shin, and both extended-range medium lasers struck his torso and sent a flash of amber warning lights onto his command console.

Declan ignored them and pressed forward into the next street to block his opponent's line of sight, then he ran down two blocks and cut sharply to the left down a nearby alleyway. When he cut left again, he found the *Sha Yu* right where he wanted it, facing straight ahead, hoping to cut him off when he slowly rounded the corner.

Declan fired his Gauss rifle, and the supersonic slug shattered control runs in the *Sha Yu*'s nearest arm, causing it to droop, and his pair of medium lasers burrowed straight through the 'Mech's torso. The *Sha Yu* turned, hoping to get its own weapons to bear, but Declan was too quick. He launched a flurry of short-range missiles and shot another Gauss rifle round into the Capellan 'Mech. This slug blasted through the extra-light engine in the torso, and the heat bloom that followed lit up on his infrared sensors. Declan lined up for a follow-up shot, but a PPC beam from outside his line of sight skewered the *Sha Yu*'s damaged torso, destroying the fusion engine and sending the 'Mech to the ground with a resounding crash.

Now that he had a second to breathe, Declan switched back to the other channel. "Darryl, how you holding up?"

"Things are looking tight, lad. We've several 'Mechs down, and all of us are running low on supplies." For the first time in Declan's memory, Darryl sounded harried and weary. "I'm glad you're here, but I'm not too sure what you're gonna be able to do."

"We can help with that," Maeve said, cutting into the channel. "I have a Savior repair vehicle with a mobile field base on the way, and a J-37 ordnance transport. If we can hold them off long enough, you'll be able to get back in fighting shape."

"That's a lot of good hardware, lass, but can you spare it?" Darryl sounded relieved, but his voice still wavered with concern.

"We have to," the Knight replied, surprising Declan as well. "Because our next step is to bring the fight to their doorstep."

Maeve Stirling was as good as her word. The repair vehicle and ordnance transports arrived quickly, escorted by no less than the remaining Grey Watch 'Mechs from the Castle. The Highlanders reinforcements moved quickly to secure the line between Warrior House Imarra's lines and the residential district, providing a buffer between the two forces as they prepared to re-engage.

From the cockpit of Taggart's *Osprey*, Declan watched the first group of reinforcements arrive; they mostly comprised the nearest Grey Watch lances and some of the quicker Hastati BattleMechs that the Castle could spare. In the distance he spotted his grandfather's *Marauder*, although he saw no other Grey Watch officers.

As if thinking it made it so, Seamus' voice came over the main comm channel: "Highlanders, we have contacts! Prepare to engage."

Declan quickly checked his secondary screen and pulled the tactical data his grandfather was sending out on the secondary channel. From the look of things, House Imarra's warriors were finally ready to engage, and had begun moving forward as a unit.

Seamus' voice switched from the main channel to the private one reserved for their use. "Dec, one of our lances covering Hamden Street is taking heavy fire. Can you assist?"

"On my way."

Declan throttled his *Osprey* into a run while his grandfather laid down a blistering storm of fire down the main thoroughfare. While the last thing he wanted to do was to abandon Seamus, he knew that not only was his 'Mech faster than many of the other Highlanders BattleMechs on the field at the moment, but he also carried significantly heavier and more advanced weaponry.

Taking the final turn onto Hamden Street, he saw a full lance of House Imarra BattleMechs engaged with the remains of a Grey Watch lance that had blocked the road, keeping the Imarra 'Mechs from entering the residential district. The largest Grey Watch 'Mech, an immense *Atlas*, stood against all comers, lashing out with its long-range missiles at one of the Capellan attackers.

"*Osprey*, this is Halloran. Welcome to the party."

The quick message was all Declan needed to recognize the now-familiar *Atlas*. He had not known Lieutenant Colonel Halloran was a member of the Grey Watch, but now that he thought about it, the idea made sense. If the Grey Watch needed a surreptitious source of equipment, ammunition, and personnel, a senior instructor at the NMA would be the perfect contact for that...

The thought made something click in the back of Declan's mind, but he would worry about it later, after the battle.

If Halloran was distracted by Declan's arrival, he did not show it; he fired sequential beams from his medium lasers as the House Imarra forces closed the distance, hoping to drag him down with sheer weight of numbers. At his side, using the *Atlas'* higher profile as cover, Cathy Glazier's *Rifleman* alternated fire between her large lasers and autocannons to keep her heat down, providing additional firepower against the Capellan onslaught. A trail of smoke farther down the intersection showed where another member of the Grey Watch lance had fallen, but Declan could not identify it from this distance.

Taking a position beside the *Atlas*, Declan fired his Gauss rifle, which took an approaching *Vindicator* in the chest. Despite the heavy damage, the Capellan BattleMech continued forward until Halloran's *Atlas* bracketed it with a half-dozen short-range missiles; explosions cratered the *Vindicator's* armor, forcing the 'Mech to momentarily halt its advance.

Declan triggered his comms. "Knight One, this is Knight Four. We have a major push on Hamden Street. Requesting reinforcements."

The long pause before Maeve's response told him all he needed to know about the viciousness of the fighting at her location. "Negative, Knight Four. All forces are heavily engaged."

"Understood." Declan cut the connection and focused on the approaching BattleMechs.

A pair of Imarra BattleMechs, a *Koschei* and *Sha Yu*, rushed down the wide street, weaving around each other as much as the space would allow. Both 'Mechs lashed out with their lasers, striking the *Atlas* across the torso and left arm. Declan launched a brace of missiles at the *Sha Yu*, but most of them struck a nearby industrial building as his target increased speed.

Cathy's *Rifleman* stepped out of the *Atlas'* shadow to fire at the smaller 'Mechs, but that was just what the Imarra warriors had been waiting for. At nearly the same time, a *Catapult II* emerged from the shadow of a nearby building and launched forty long-range missiles at the *Rifleman*. The Grey Watch 'Mech seemed to disappear into a pall of smoke, and when the cloud dissipated, one of the *Rifleman's* arms was dangling uselessly. Declan sent a Gauss rifle round back in return, smashing the *Catapult II* across its beak-like torso before it ducked back behind a nearby building.

Seeking to capitalize on the damage caused by their lancemate, the two Imarra MechWarriors fired their weapons at Cathy's *Rifleman*, which was just an instant too slow returning to cover. The two BattleMechs' lasers cut deep rents into the larger 'Mech's armor. An instant later, an autocannon burst from the *Koschei* hammered deep into the *Rifleman's* torso. The autocannon ammo there touched off into a chain of secondary explosions that ripped off the *Rifleman's* other arm and sent Cathy's 'Mech to the ground, unmoving.

The small victory was fleeting, however, as Halloran fired back with his heavy autocannon and sawed off the *Sha Yu's* leg, sending the enemy 'Mech crashing to the ground. The *Koschei* attempted to provide cover for its lancemate, but Declan's pair of extended-range medium lasers caused it to duck down a nearby alleyway while Halloran's *Atlas* finished off the smaller 'Mech with its own medium lasers.

Having scared off the attackers for a brief moment, Declan turned to check on Cathy when his comm buzzed again.

"*Osprey*, one of my lancemates is in trouble on the next street. Can you assist?"

"Affirmative," Declan replied, realizing Halloran didn't recognize his voice, and he brought up the positioning data the other man had sent him. Lighting his jump jets, he took to the sky, leaping over a pair of nearby buildings to where the coordinates led.

In an instant, he saw the issue: another pair of House Imarra BattleMechs, a *Wraith* and a *Yao Lien*, had cornered a Grey Watch *Wolverine*. It was painted in black and white to resemble it wearing a tuxedo, which meant it could only belong to Tux. While normally an extremely nimble medium 'Mech, Tux's *Wolverine* showed damage to one of its jump jets, and the newer Confederation machines had trapped it.

Landing off to one side of the ambushers, Declan fired all of his weapons at the nearest target, the *Wraith*. His Gauss rifle shattered the sloped armor over the 'Mech's hip, and his medium lasers and missiles scored damage all across its side, sending it crashing into the building. Seeing the opportunity, Tux's *Wolverine* cut through the *Wraith*'s already-damaged hip armor with his autocannon and lasers, severing the left leg entirely.

Seemingly unconcerned about their lancemate, the Imarra *Yao Lien* fired both of its snub-nose PPCs at Declan, washing the other 'Mech with man-made lightning. Declan fought with his controls to keep the *Osprey* upright, but the sudden loss of over a ton of armor caused him to fall backward.

The *Yao Lien* was on him in an instant, firing its PPCs as quickly as they could cycle. The next shot sheared his Gauss rifle off, and Declan had just enough time to gasp in a breath as he struggled to get back to his feet.

But a single kick from the Imarra MechWarrior sent his *Osprey* back down to the ground, and he looked up to see the *Yao Lien* leveling its arm at his cockpit.

Suddenly, his vision was blocked as the *Wolverine* stepped in front of him and unleashed an alpha strike just before the *Yao Lien* could fire its PPCs again. From his angle, Declan watched the autocannon and medium laser cut deeply into the Capellan 'Mech's chest, and Tux's short-range missiles struck the chest and head.

Unfortunately, the damage was not enough to keep the *Yao Lien* from firing, and the critically damaged *Wolverine* crumpled, no longer under human control.

Getting his feet back under him, Declan lashed out with his remaining weapons. His extended-range medium lasers lanced deeper into the damage the *Wolverine* had wrought. A visible spike of heat showed on his infrared sensors as he cracked the *Yao Lien*'s engine shielding, and then the 'Mech slumped over, shut down from overheating. The Capellan MechWarrior bailed out, their ejection seat rocketing itself quickly out of view.

Declan spared a brief moment to say a brief prayer for Tux, the brave *Wolverine* pilot who had saved his life, and then rushed down the street to where Halloran was still holding the line.

He arrived just in time to see the massive *Atlas* fall.

During his engagement with the other Capellan BattleMechs, the *Atlas* had sustained critical damage from the approaching Imarra forces. The *Koschei* lay crumpled at the *Atlas'* feet, but one arm was missing, and the armor across the skull-faced assault 'Mech's front had been ripped open in countless places, leaving gaping rents all over.

As he rushed back into the fray, Declan saw a swarm of long-range missiles fly overhead and strike the *Atlas* in a dozen places. He would never know which warhead sneaked inside the 'Mech's torso, but one must have touched off some of the remaining ammo there. Internal explosions wracked the Grey Watch BattleMech, sending it crumpling bonelessly to the ground.

Feeling suddenly very alone, Declan stepped into the thoroughfare and squared off against the approaching Capellan forces, his hands tightening instinctively on his joysticks as he lowered his crosshairs on the closest enemy BattleMech.

"Clear the road, man!" an unfamiliar voice ordered.

Declan momentarily froze as a large laser fired to one side of him, followed by the telltale bluish-white flash of a PPC. Cutting sharply to his right, he swiveled his torso to see a lance of fresh Grey Watch BattleMechs take up positions in the intersection where Halloran had fallen.

Turning back to the Capellans to help with the assault, he was unsurprised to see the enemy clearing the road, pulling back to regroup. Under the cover of the Highlanders' weapons, Declan ran back to the intersection and took his place beside a familiar *Marauder* that stood sentinel over the fallen *Atlas*.

Declan spared a glance downward, saying another silent prayer for a fallen warrior. His eyes then slid over to the ruined *Rifleman* just beyond it. "Cathy?"

Seamus' voice was softer than Declan ever remembered hearing it. "I'm sorry, lad."

Declan nodded, fighting the rage welling up in his chest. "Tux, too."

"Ah, Tux. Wasnae much of a talker, but was never late to chow call. He will be missed."

"He saved my life," Declan confessed, his gaze returning to the alleyway where the *Wolverine* had fallen.

"We will remember him," Seamus vowed, and then turned his *Marauder* toward the *Osprey*. "For now, ye need to get back to the Castle. We've got things from here."

Declan began to protest, but Seamus cut him off. "Dinna bother arguing. Ye're missing over half of yer armor, and yer most potent weapon. Ye're no use to us dead, and the Highlanders are here now. We've blunted their attack. Now it is up to ye ta help finish this thing."

Declan was silent for a long moment, and then nodded, throttling up the *Osprey* to a run as he plotted the most efficient course back to the Castle.

Yes, he would finish this...

For Halloran. For Cathy. For Tux.

For Taggart.

For all of them.

CHAPTER 9

"The Capellan media liaison is informing us that House Imarra troops are being redeployed to protect the residential quarter of the city, following credible reports of Highlanders 'Mechs being seen in the area. The liaison recommends all citizens of Tara remain in their homes for their own safety..."

—Tegan Shea, *Northwind Today*, 9 December 3150

HPG COMPOUND
TARA, NORTHWIND
REPUBLIC OF THE SPHERE
9 DECEMBER 3150

"*Shiao-zhang* Garzon, would you be so kind as to tell me what the hell you are doing?"

From the pickup on the small screen in her office, Lindsey Baxter could see House Imarra's acting House Master communicating from the cockpit of his BattleMech, a four-legged *Trebaruna*. Having just heard about the mobilization of a significant portion of the Warrior House's troops from their defensive positioning around Kohler Spaceport, Lindsey had headed to her office to have a quiet chat with the other commander.

When Garzon spoke, his voice was carefully measured, unaffected by her open irritation. "I am currently in the process of hunting down the Grey Watch forces that attacked *Gao-shiao-zhang* Hui and *Sang-shao* Qiao," he replied. "I received actionable intelligence that informed me of Grey Watch forces hiding near Tara's residential areas, which required me to move immediately to halt a potential threat to both my command and our tactical objectives."

And I bet I know where you received that "actionable intelligence," Lindsey thought.

"And this intel just happened to bring you to the doorstep of the residential areas of the city?" She fought to keep her own voice neutral. "A location which just happens to put a significant amount of your troops within striking range of a target the Highlanders will defend at all costs?"

"It is well within my patrol area, and my area of control, *Sang-shao*. We have already engaged forces conclusively identified as belonging to the Grey Watch, and that should more than confirm the necessity of my actions."

Lindsey kept a tolerant expression on her face, although internally she seethed. Unfortunately, there was only so much she could say at this point. The Warrior Houses' traditional autonomy, coupled with actionable intelligence from the planet's Maskirovka liaison, would make for a strong case for the *shiao-zhang*'s actions. Coupled with the fact that he surely had battleROM footage of the engagement with Highlanders forces, any complaints she made now would seem petty at best; at worst, it would be seen as an attempt to cover her own blindness at allowing enemy forces to hide in an area she had declared tacitly off limits.

No, there is little I can do about this for now. She nodded curtly. "Understood, *Shiao-zhang*. What is your current status?"

"I am bringing up additional forces to counter an anticipated counterstrike. My scouts have reported additional enemy reinforcements en route from the Castle, and my forces are ready to engage." He gave her an ingratiating smile. "You may wish to contact *Sang-shao* Qiao and have her prepare for a strike at the Castle. If we succeed in drawing away a significant portion of the enemy from their defensive positions, Laurel's Legion should be able to strike while they are weakened."

As much as Lindsey loathed to admit it, Garzon was right. The Highlanders could not afford to leave the residential district of Tara unprotected, and even if the Republic forces balked at leaving their redoubt, the Highlanders never would.

Swallowing her pride, she gave a sharp nod. "I will inform her, *Shiao-zhang*. Please keep me apprised."

Garzon nodded and cut the signal, while Lindsey took a moment to pound her fist on her desk. Rising to her feet, she stalked to her door and headed into her command center at the HPG compound. She waved off the guards who stiffened to attention as she walked in, and turned to Jacobs, the officer she had left in charge so she could speak privately with Garzon.

"Jacobs, please contact *Sang-shao* Qiao, and have her go to Condition Gold and prepare her forces for immediate deployment. Warrior House Imarra has engaged with Highlanders forces within the city, and we may have an opportunity to strike at the Castle."

Jacobs confirmed the order and moved to his console to send the message. While Lindsey would have preferred to send the message herself, she knew she had a far more important message to send, one only she could do.

"Ms. Haller, please get *Sho-sho* Ikeda on the comm," Lindsey ordered, and the young ComStar technician immediately complied. To Bianca's credit, it only took her a few minutes to get the Kuritan commander on the line, through no fault of her own, but every moment only served to darken Lindsey's mood.

"*Sang-shao* Baxter," Ikeda said, giving her a bland smile. "I was not expecting another message until tomorrow. I heard there was a battle within the city? I hope there was no lasting damage to your units."

For a brief moment, Lindsey wondered just how much the man knew, but she merely bowed her head at the quality of his intelligence. "My compliments on your intel, *Sho-sho*," she replied. "My forces have moved to draw out some of the Highlanders from the Castle in a bid to finally end the Republic threat to our interests in Tara."

"A move long overdue," the Kuritan officer responded, keeping his voice neutral. "I applaud your efforts."

Her eyes narrowed at the thinly veiled criticism. She knew he was intentionally goading her, hoping to reinforce whatever mental conceptions he had of female warriors, but she refused to take the bait.

"I believe we would be far more successful in our efforts if you would agree to assist us in an assault on the Castle," she replied. "Laurel's Legion is prepared to strike while the enemy is weakened, and with your support we could deny the Republic their final bastion on the planet."

Ikeda nodded, but in consideration rather than agreement. From Lindsey's position, it was the best of all worlds: the Kuritan forces could drop near or onto the Castle, depending on their preference, which would force the remaining Republic troops to split their attention between Ikeda's warriors and Laurel's Legion. Even if the joint task force was initially unsuccessful in taking the Castle from the Republic, the Highlanders were engaged with Warrior House Imarra, and the Castle would be unable to send reinforcements; thus, Lindsey herself would be able to split off some of her own detachments to finish off the Highlanders once and for all. With the assistance of her Unity Pact allies, she would finally be able to complete the mission the Chancellor himself had given her.

However, a quick victory was only achievable if Ikeda agreed to finally *do* something.

"I can certainly see how this would benefit your current situation," Ikeda said, and she watched him warily. "My major concern, however, is tactical coordination. You currently have your troops split between three widely separated areas of control, and I am concerned that bringing my warriors down on a fourth vector would be the best tactical choice."

Lindsey attempted to keep her expression calm, despite wanting to grit her teeth. The worst part of Ikeda's statement was that he was correct: between FOB Romeo, Tara's residential sector, and the HPG compound, her regiments were separated from each other by a significant distance, and coordination between them and the Combine troops would be a challenge at best.

She also did not blame him for being concerned about her intentions. From a purely pragmatic standpoint, if her forces were even slightly late to the battle, the Republic might fall onto the Kuritan forces with a vengeance, risking defeat in detail between the Kuritans and Laurel's Legion.

Not to mention, she was also certain that Ikeda wondered if this was all a trap on her own part, to get his forces to engage the Republic while the Legion was still en route, only for her to pull her troops at the last moment. Such a maneuver would preserve the Capellan forces while driving the Republic and

Combine troops into open conflict that would free up Lindsey's own tactical and strategic options.

She prepared to give the Kuritan commander a convincing breakdown of why it would be in his best interest to assist when she noticed Cheng step into her sightline. From just outside of the monitor's camera range, he gave her a knowing look, and she took the opportunity to momentarily halt the conversation.

"Pardon me for a moment, *Sho-sho*. I am getting an update from one of my staff."

She signaled to cut off the channel before Ikeda could respond, nodding thanks to Bianca as she turned to Cheng, who stepped down into the command area. The Maskirovka operative watched her coolly, clearly displeased at the thought of being considered only a member of her staff.

"Yes, Mr. Cheng?" she asked, her voice taut with surprised anger. She was an officer in the CCAF, and she refused to let this man get to her.

"*Sang-shao.*" Cheng's voice was pitched low enough that no one around could hear them. "I think I might be able to assist you with the Kuritans."

Lindsey carefully scanned his face for any sign he was looking to capitalize on her lack of success with the Kuritan officer. Seeing that he actually looked sincere, she gave a small nod. "At this point, I am willing to try new things. What are you thinking?"

"Before the *gao-shiao-zhang* was injured, we had been discussing the possibility of someone going up to the Kuritan fleet to parley with them in person."

Lindsey nodded. "The *gao-shiao-zhang* and I had discussed the possibility when the Kuritan forces first reached orbit, but at the time I needed to remain close to the action here in Tara." Her chest tightened for a moment as she thought of Hui lying wounded in his hospital bed. "Unfortunately, my necessity to remain here has only increased with everything that has happened."

"And rightly so," Cheng replied. "With the *gao-shiao-zhang* wounded, it is all the more vital that you should be remain to lead our counterattack when the time comes. However, I was actually volunteering my own services."

Lindsey managed to keep the surprise from her face. "*You* would travel up to the Kuritan fleet? I am not sure I like the thought of you being in the hands of allies who have proven so reluctant to come to our assistance."

"I would not normally recommend it either, but I fear our recent intel makes it all the more imperative that we ascertain the intentions of our allies as soon as possible. I agree with you that steps must be taken immediately to neutralize the Republic threat. And the best way to do that is to convince Ikeda to intervene on our side, and quickly."

"And you think you can succeed where I have failed?"

If he had been thinking it, he was tactful enough to not let it show in his expression. "Respectfully, Ikeda's Hikage warriors are traditionally DEST-trained, which makes them far more like the Maskirovka than a unit like yours. I am hoping to prevail on our shared background to get a better idea of their intentions, if not get them to assist directly. I intend to bring them updates from our less-recent intelligence briefings, giving them some new data to process, but nothing that might compromise our own active operations."

"And if they capture you? I am loath to give up my main intelligence asset."

"If they do, then you will certainly know their intentions," Cheng replied with a thin smile. "Not to mention, my own resources are considerable. I trust the Kuritans no more than you do. However, I believe it is vital for our current operations that we know how to move forward." He shrugged. "In the best-case scenario, they agree to come down from orbit, either as a diversion to push the Republic into a trap of our own choosing, or to actively assist us in eradicating the last vestiges of Northwind's defenders."

Of course, neither said that in the worst-case scenario, Cheng would be tortured for his most recent intelligence data, including information about the Capellan troops.

As much as she disliked letting the agent out of her sight, her mind was awash with possibilities. She knew Cheng had been talking with Hui's second-in-command, and she knew Warrior House Imarra's recent redistribution of forces had been partially his work. With him out of the way, she could likely prevail on *Shiao-zhang* Garzon to rethink his actions and convince him there was a better way forward than threatening the people of Tara.

Not to mention, there was always the slim chance that Cheng would be successful.

"All right," she said. "I don't like it, but it might be our best plan. You're approved to leave immediately." Lindsey turned back to the communications console. "Bianca, could you please raise the *sho-sho* again?"

This time, it took the ComStar adept a little longer to reestablish the connection, although Lindsey did not doubt it was just Ikeda's power play to make sure she knew that he was not merely waiting by his comm console for her response. When he did come back on the line, he wore an expression of patient tolerance.

"I hope everything goes well with you, *Sang-shao*," Ikeda responded.

"Of course, *Sho-sho*. I believe we may have an opportunity to finally deal with the Republic resistance on Northwind. Would you permit my intelligence liaison to come up and speak with you personally?"

Ikeda glanced over at Cheng and smiled slightly. "It would be an honor to meet with a member of the famed Maskirovka like Agent Cheng." Neither Lindsey nor Cheng revealed their surprise that Ikeda knew Cheng by name. "Will you require me to send down a transport?"

"I have an ST-46 shuttle at my disposal," Cheng said. "I can reach you within the hour."

"I shall look forward to it," Ikeda replied, and with a nod, the comm channel went blank.

Lindsey faced Cheng and gave him a careful nod. "Well, here's hoping you can find some common ground with your counterpart up there."

"As you command, *Sang-shao*."

CHAPTER 10

*"Tegan, I am here on the ground outside of the residential quarter.
For everyone just tuning in, forces of the Highlanders' Grey Watch
and the Capellan Warrior House Imarra were engaged in a vicious
battle on the outskirts of the residential sector, with both sides
claiming it was for the protection of the citizens of Tara. I am happy
to report that despite some small clusters of fighting, things seem to
have quieted down here, and... Damn it, Kyle! Get that on tape! That
will look great on—"*

—Charles Brunt, *Northwind Today*, 9 December 3150

UNION-CLASS DROPSHIP *BLISTERING WIND*
GEOSYNCHRONOUS ORBIT
NORTHWIND
REPUBLIC OF THE SPHERE
9 DECEMBER 3150

Sho-sho Hisao Ikeda glanced up from his console as *Chu-sa* Ivan Hallow
stepped up beside him. In the microgravity environment, Hallow's magnetic
boots allowed him to stay firmly planted at his commander's side.

"*Sho-sho*, would you like me to receive our guests?" Ivan asked.

Ikeda nodded. "Meet them at the docking collar and bring them to the
main conference room." He smiled thinly. "We will make them wait a bit to
remind them that we are not here on their timetable."

His aide gave a deep bow, nearly hiding his own fleeting smile,
and departed.

Ikeda turned his chair to face the main holotank, where the *Blistering
Wind*'s captain, Hidori Sato, sat across from him. "Captain, do we have any
additional information from the surface?"

Sato's expression turned serious. "We are prepared to take advantage
of whatever opening we see, *Sho-sho*. I have the remainder of our aerospace
fighters prepared for escort operations for our DropShips, and we have
constantly updated flight plans for combat drops on either the Castle or Tara."

Ikeda nodded. Since his DropShips were needed to ferry his troops to the surface of Northwind, he had left several fighters and a single *Leopard CV* DropShip back at the jump point to guard his JumpShips. While it was unlikely the Republic had any naval forces in the area that could jump in and threaten his retreat, he had not reached his current rank by taking anything for granted.

"All right, have—"

"Captain," a bridge technician cut in, "the Capellan shuttle has completed docking maneuvers."

Sato nodded at Ikeda, then turned to his technician. "Please inform them to—"

The world heaved.

Ikeda was flung against his seat restraints and struck his head against the back of his chair as everything shuddered and quaked around him. He tasted copper. Red flashing lights strobed throughout the room as emergency klaxons shrieked, notifying all personnel and passengers that something terrible had occurred.

"Status report!" the captain hollered, having barely caught himself against the holotank. When no response was forthcoming, Ikeda turned to see the damage-control officer slumped forward lifelessly, caught up in the snapped remains of the failed chair restraints, which had caused the man's head to strike his console.

As Ikeda undid his restraints and kicked off to reach the console, one of the nearby officers leaned over to analyze the readout. "We have a hull breach on Deck Four, sir. Explosive decompression pushed us out of stable orbit, and we are in a slow spin. Emergency bulkheads have activated, and damage-control teams are en route."

Sato whirled on the young officer at the conning station. "Helm, can you get us back into orbit?"

"Attempting to, sir. Port stabilizers are damaged." The helmsman's hair was plastered down to his skull with a fine sheen of sweat, his hands working the controls like a master pianist. "We may have to attempt an emergency landing."

Ikeda turned to Sato, his eyes intent. "Were we attacked? How did they get close enough?"

The captain did not respond, his concentration completely on getting his ship back under control. "Sensors?"

"No enemy ships on screen, sir... Wait... Multiple contacts coming up from the surface: Capellan fighters!"

A sudden, yawning feeling struck Ikeda in his chest. "Where is the Capellan shuttle?"

The young officer who'd taken over the damage control station responded. "The shuttle is destroyed, sir. Heavy damage at the docking collar cut our sensors in that area."

Instantly, Ikeda knew what had happened. "Captain, get our fighters out to intercept the Capellans! This was a trap!"

Sato whirled on him, his eyes hard, as the realization struck him as well. They stared at each other wordlessly for a moment, then Sato turned to the tactical officer. "All craft, all craft, launch your ready fighters and intercept the Capellan forces! You are weapons free!"

The orders were relayed over the din, and once again the speaker screeched: "Bridge, Engineering. We have partially stabilized our orbit, but I cannot confirm for how long. We need extensive repairs before we are fully spaceworthy again."

"*Sho-sa*," Sato said calmly, "can we manage reentry?"

There was a long, desperate pause. "I don't know, Captain."

"*Know, Sho-sa!*" Ikeda cut in. "We are going to pay back these treacherous Capellan bastards in the only way they know! Communications, get me..."

His voice caught in his throat as he remembered...

Deck Four.

The docking collar...

Ivan.

Ikeda squeezed his eyes shut for a moment and slammed his fist against the console as he fought back tears of rage. The pain brought him back to reality, and he felt an ache in his jaw from where he had been clenching it. "Captain, have all fighters intercept the Capellan forces! All DropShips, rig for anti-fighter operations! I want the sky cleared of this dishonorable scum!"

His eyes locked on the screen as the two opposing aerofighter swarms lashed out from long range and began dogfighting, a lightning-quick series of parries and lunges at supersonic speeds. Ballistic and energy weapons rippled along in a storm of sheer viciousness, interspersed only by the occasional brief flash as a fighter exploded, the last of the oxygen in the cockpit burning up as the void claimed it.

The helmsman turned to Sato, his breathing returning to normal. "Captain, I have returned us to a stable orbit, and we are holding steady near our final position."

"Excellent!" Sato replied. "Engineering, status?"

"The emergency bulkheads have sealed off the damaged sections, and we are effecting emergency repairs on the stabilizer. Anything more will require a spacewalk."

The captain nodded, and Ikeda saw the wheels in his mind turning. Now that they were back into their orbit, they could hold out for some time, even with the stabilizer working at less than full efficiency. No one would relish going outside in the middle of a vicious space battle, especially knowing a single emergency maneuver could throw them off from the ship, leaving them to float in the void until their oxygen ran out.

"Damage control." For a moment, Ikeda could not recognize his own voice. "Were there any survivors from the hull breach?"

"No, sir," the damage-control officer replied cautiously. "The emergency bulkheads were triggered instantly at decompression... The entire section was lost before manuals could be put into place."

Ikeda's eyes threatened to squeeze shut again, but he merely focused on the blood-red section of the damage-control chart on his monitor. In case of an emergency or during battle, the outermost bulkheads on the ship were programmed to drop like a guillotine at the first sign of decompression. It was a desperate safety measure for situations like this, where a sudden loss of atmosphere could threaten the entire ship. It was one of the reasons all spacers moved through the hatches so quickly...there was no warning, no klaxon ahead of time. The single duty of these emergency bulkheads was to protect as many people as possible, and if you were caught on the wrong side, or worse, below one as it snapped shut...well, every spacer had a tale about such things.

"Engineering." Once again, Ikeda found his voice. "How quickly can we prepare for descent?"

Sato's head shot up incredulously, and even the voice on the other side of the intercom hesitated. "Sir?"

Ikeda ignored him. "Engineering, how quickly can we make planetfall?"

"The stabilizer is space-only, sir. Our descent profile will be affected by the hull damage, but we should be able to compensate for it."

Ikeda nodded, remembering from his own DropShip training years ago that the areas nearest the docking collars were some of the most heavily reinforced regions of the ship, since they might be under tremendous stress in zero-g combat situations or when loading or unloading shuttles.

"Planetfall is achievable at any time, sir." The engineer allowed a small trace of humor to leak into his voice. "Staying up was the hard part. Down we can do at your command."

"Good." Ikeda turned toward Sato as he straightened in his chair. "Captain, I want these Capellans dealt with, and then I want immediate preparation for Deployment Plan Theta."

Sato, to his credit, only gave a sharp nod, affirming the orders, and began calling out preparations to his crew. Deployment Plan Theta was a contingency in which he could not easily wrest the HPG from the Capellans. Unlike his other plans, which capitalized on lightning drops close enough to threaten the Republic forces, Theta dropped them on the far side of Tara, forcing the Capellans to split their focus between three different points of hostile contact: Ikeda's landing site, the Castle, and the Northwind Military Academy. Even with the sheer number of BattleMechs the Capellan forces could field, such a situation would have them caught between a rock and a hard place, and would certainly not be well received.

Having finished giving his orders, the captain stepped up beside Ikeda. "Sir," he said, careful not to allow his voice to be overheard, "I understand your desire, but we have been heavily damaged. Descending at this time—"

"Captain." Ikeda's voice was calmer than he expected, more reasonable than he had ever felt. He would often rage at any black-navy officer who dared debate his orders, but something dark and cold had settled inside him, and he could almost feel the presence of his murdered aide behind him. Hallow had always gone to great lengths to ensure that his commander, brilliant as he was, always knew of the additional concerns in any situation, and now that he was gone, Ikeda was going to have to rely on himself.

"Captain, I understand your concerns...but understand mine: the honor of the Dragon has been besmirched by the treacherous actions of our supposed allies. Our Coordinator offered them a pact against the Republic, and these

Capellans, whether at the behest of their own leader or on their own authority, have struck at us in treacherous fashion. The blood of the Dragon is on their hands, and I will not allow this to stand. We will seize the HPG they covet for the bounty of the Dragon, and then we will move to wipe every single one of their BattleMechs from the face of the planet."

Sato reared back slightly from the intensity of Ikeda's response, and the rest of the bridge crew was carefully listening to every word.

"With that in mind, *Captain*—" Ikeda stressed the other man's rank carefully. "—it is my desire that we get down to the ground as quickly and safely as we can, and then complete our mission as I have just outlined it."

The captain bowed silently, and then turned to the rest of the bridge crew. His orders came out in rapid sequence, and preparations began for the first phases of the drop.

Turning back to the holotank, Ikeda saw the Capellan aerospace forces beginning to retreat. To his intense pleasure, the displays showed that less than 40 percent of the attacking Capellan fighters remained, and several were trailing atmosphere and debris as they returned to the planet, his remaining fighters hot on their heels. For the briefest of moments, he considered contacting the Republic countess to let her know her Capellan foes were weakened, but instantly thought better of it. If Countess Campbell was wise enough to see the opportunity and capitalize on it, she deserved to, but she had done nothing yet to help with his mission, and he was wary of putting his faith in another so soon after the most recent betrayal.

As he watched, the other four DropShips in his task force maneuvered into drop formation, in preparation to swoop down from the sky and disgorge the might of the Dragon's fist. He informed Sato he would prepare for the drop from the cockpit of his 'Mech, spared one final glance at the last spot he had seen Ivan alive, then ducked through the bridge's hatch so quickly it nearly touched his shoulders.

The time had come for the Dragon to show its might, and *Sho-sho* Hisao Ikeda was determined to be the one to do it.

CHAPTER 11

"Citizens of Northwind, this is Tegan Shea with a breaking news announcement. We have received word of an explosion aboard one of the Draconis Combine DropShips, and Capellan and Combine aerospace forces have engaged in space over the planet. We will continue to update you as we receive more information on this breaking story."

—Tegan Shea, *Northwind Today*, 9 December 3150

CAPELLAN ALLIED COMMAND CENTER
HPG COMPOUND
TARA, NORTHWIND
REPUBLIC OF THE SPHERE
9 DECEMBER 3150

Upon hearing the alarm klaxons going off within the compound, Lindsey shot up from her desk and was halfway to her office door when her wrist comm began beeping.

"Status report," she demanded.

"We are registering a massive explosion on the Kuritan flagship," Newsom responded. "It has suffered extensive hull and stabilizer damage, but the crew managed to regain control."

Once inside the command center, she headed down to the main command well. "Comms, can you raise Mr. Cheng's shuttle?"

"No response, sir," Newsom said from his console. "Our sensors readings show the explosion was near where the shuttle had docked."

A half-dozen possibilities ran through her mind in a moment. *Did the Republic forces somehow manage to sneak a bomb onto Cheng's ship to negate our intelligence advantage?* If this was all a coordinated counterintelligence action, the recent attacks on *Sang-shao* Qiao and the *gao-shiao-zhang* needed to be considered in a completely different light. *Was this all an orchestrated effort to behead our command structure?*

Or was it a step further? If the shuttle exploded, it might have killed Ikeda and Cheng, vital parts of the Capellan and Kurita leadership. Such a step might have meant a deathblow for both of the allied forces in the system and allow the Republic the opportunity to strike at them when the losses left them disorganized.

Lindsey pulled herself free from her thoughts and turned to Newsom. "Send a message to the Kuritan forces, see if they require assistance. While we await their response, launch the Cap Fives. I want them in the air and tracking the Kuritan DropShip."

"No response from the *Blistering Wind*, *Sang-shao*."

"Then get me the commodore."

Newsom made the connection. From the grim expression on the face in the holovid transmission, Commodore Xio, the senior naval commander for the Capellan expedition to Northwind, had already been tracking the situation from his DropShip, which was berthed at Tara's spaceport. "*Sang-shao*, we are reading an explosion in orbit, but have only limited data. Can we get an update?"

"That was on the Kuritan flagship," Lindsey replied. "Can we get assistance to them?"

"I have one of the DropShips spooling up right now. It is going to be tight, but I believe we can intercept before they hit the ground." The commodore's expression was taut. "If not, we can be there for search and rescue."

Lindsey was already in motion, ordering the command channel opened to the other Capellan force leaders. In rapid succession Centrella-Tompkins, Qiao, and Garzon appeared on the main screen.

"We just recorded an explosion on the Kuritan flagship," she told them, "and it is currently on a minimally controlled path to the ground. I have the commodore scrambling our aerospace assets to assist, but if this was a covert attack perpetrated by the Republic, we need to prepare. I want all units brought to readiness level Orange. We must prepare for a full-scale assault." She looked at her fellow commanders before continuing. "Agent Cheng had just docked his shuttle with the *Blistering Wind*, and that appears to be the target of the explosion. At this time, Agent Cheng is considered MIA."

Qiao and Centrella-Tompkins nodded, but *Shiao-zhang* Garzon, from the camera in his BattleMech cockpit, looked obstinate. "*Sang-shao*, it may have slipped your mind, but my forces are already engaged with the Republic."

Lindsey's eyes narrowed at his response, and she straightened, clasping her hands behind her back. "I assure you, *Shiao-zhang*, the information has most certainly not slipped my mind. My primary duty is to maintain the safety and security of the HPG compound, not to engage in reprisals against the people of Northwind."

She was ready to say more, but a technician from behind cut in. "*Sang-shao*, we are receiving a transmission from the *Blistering Wind*."

"Put it through," Lindsey ordered, ending the other call with a sharp nod.

It took only a moment, and Ikeda's face was visible on the holoscreen, his normally perfect hair now mussed and out of place.

"*Sho-sho*, we just registered an explosion on your vessel. Are you—"

"*Treachery!*" Ikeda growled venomously, turning the word into a curse. "Is this the way you treat your allies?"

Lindsey straightened, her expression confused. "*Sho-sho*, surely you do not believe that we—"

"We have conclusive proof that the explosion that damaged my DropShip came from your shuttle, and there was only a single pilot on board when it docked." Ikeda's anger was palpable. "The explosion killed over a dozen members of my crew, including my aide. Their blood calls out for vengeance, and I intend to give it to them."

Cheng... Lindsey managed to keep a scowl from her face. *What did you do?*

"*Sho-sho*," she said, "you must know I would never condone an attack against your vessel. We are your allies."

"*No more*," Ikeda responded, the unbridled hate in his eyes visible even through the holodisplay. "This is exactly the sort of treachery I should have expected from the Capellan Confederation. You have betrayed our pact, and now you shall reap the whirlwind. Prepare yourselves." With a violent motion, the communication cut off.

Lindsey turned to Newsom, about to order him to get the Kuritan officer back on the line, but immediately thought better of it. "Bring back the others," she said, and in moments her fellow commanders returned to the screen. "I have just spoken with *Sho-sho* Ikeda. He believes we are to blame for the attack on his vessel, and I believe he intends to attack."

"That is ludicrous!" Qiao replied. "He cannot possibly think we had anything to do with it."

"Apparently he disagrees. Regardless of what he believes, we need to respond to what he does. I am ordering all commands to Condition Red. Prepare for immediate combat."

The other commanders confirmed the order, and Centrella-Tompkins and Garzon dropped off the screen. Qiao remained a few seconds longer, giving Lindsey a nod of support before signing off.

Lindsey took a moment to stare at the dark screen and then called out for a member of her security detail.

"Yes, *Sang-shao*?" the officer replied, stepping forward briskly.

"I have reason to believe Agent Cheng was not on the shuttle that docked with the *Blistering Wind*. Find him and bring him to me immediately."

With that, she pulled up the positioning maps for the various commands and began to prepare for imminent battle.

CHAPTER 12

"Countess, we are getting a message for you...from the Draconis Combine commander."

—Brigadier General Luis McNamara, 9 December 3150

THE CASTLE
NORTHWIND
REPUBLIC OF THE SPHERE
9 DECEMBER 3150

Declan considered it only luck that he was deep in discussion with Lady Maeve Stirling in the Castle command center when General McNamara had summoned her to observe the incoming communication from *Sho-sho* Ikeda. Despite multiple attempts, the Draconis Combine forces had refused to speak with any of the Republic leaders before now, making the change all the more startling. The news that the Capellans and Combine forces were currently fighting in orbit made the situation no less confusing.

From the upper level of the command center, Declan and Maeve looked down into the command well, where Countess Tara Campbell had initiated contact with Ikeda. The countess remained focused in front of the screen, projecting a carefully maintained facade of calm while her staff rushed around outside the camera view. Like everyone else, Tara was still not exactly sure what had just happened in orbit, as information was only slowly trickling into the command center, but she was not above taking advantage of it for the good of the Republic. "Are you all right, *Sho-sho*? We registered an explosion in orbit."

"It appears you were correct about the intent of our Capellan 'allies,'" Countess," *Sho-sho* Ikeda stated matter-of-factly, his measured tone a thin veneer over the rage that burned in his eyes. "Their shuttle, allegedly carrying a liaison to us, exploded when it docked with my vessel. We are now being engaged by Capellan fighter assets."

"Ah." From off camera, a nod from one of the sensor officers confirmed the information before Tara continued. "*Sho-sho*, we are prepared to provide assistance—"

"We do not require your assistance," the Kuritan commander replied curtly, "merely your cooperation. This message is to inform you that I am currently landing my troops just outside the city of Tara to engage the Capellan forces that have attacked us in such a treacherous fashion. I do not consider you my current target, but my warriors will not hesitate to fire on you if engaged."

"I understand, *Sho-sho*," the countess replied. "As long as you constrain your attacks to the Capellan forces, and do not put the citizens of Tara or the HPG at risk, we see no reason why we should be at odds."

Ikeda nodded curtly, and the screen blanked for a moment before showing the Kuritans' projected landing zones.

Declan looked over at Maeve, and the two shared a similar look of surprise.

Tara didn't hesitate to turn to McNamara's aide, Major Keddon, who was coordinating the information-gathering effort. "Major, can I get an update on what the hell just happened?"

Keddon glanced up from his screen, his face an unenviable mixture of confusion and annoyance, despite having expected the question. "We're still not completely sure, Countess. Twenty-eight minutes ago, a Capellan ST-46 shuttle docked with Ikeda's flagship, the *Blistering Wind*, in a planned docking maneuver. Eighty-six seconds after that, the Capellan craft exploded, causing a hull breach on the *Blistering Wind* and nearly knocking it out of orbit. The ship sustained heavy damage, but they managed to correct their orbit, and are now maintaining a stable descent that will put them right outside the northern plains on the outskirts of Tara. The rest of their DropShips are on their way down, while their fighter escorts are currently engaging the Capellan aerospace wing."

Campbell nodded. "Could it have been an accident?"

"I don't see how it could have been," Keddon replied, his expression thoughtful. "Shuttles do not usually carry much in the way of explosive equipment, certainly nothing that could breach the hull of a military DropShip on its own. That thing must have been loaded with explosives to have that sort of effect."

"Well, not all Capellans are known for their subtlety," the countess replied. "Major, I have a better question: why is the *Blistering Wind* still there? Shouldn't an explosion like that have destroyed it entirely?"

Keddon nodded. "I am running some simulations now, but I believe the inner airlock had not been open when the blast occurred. The explosion still breached the hull, but the armor took a greater percentage of the concussive force than it would have if they had waited. If the hatch had been open, it probably would have split the DropShip like an egg."

Maeve stepped down to the main deck, glancing over at the countess. "That points toward the explosion being on a timer, rather than a manual detonator. Could someone have slipped explosives on board without the crew knowing?"

The major considered that for a moment and nodded. "It's certainly possible, my lady. And it would make the most sense. If the shuttle were truly loaded to the gills with explosives, it would have easily crippled Ikeda's ship. I am assuming the culprits used whatever explosives they could get away with."

Could there be multiple factions in the Liao camp? Declan thought, but he didn't ask the question out loud, knowing the answer did not matter for now.

The countess was already in motion, moving deeper into the command well. "Major Keddon, sound the ready alert. Get me the unit commanders on the main channel."

It took only a moment to get the various commanders on the screen, and Maeve stepped up beside the countess as General McNamara entered the room and jointed them.

Tara immediately brought McNamara up to speed. "It seems someone has kicked the hornet's nest. We don't know who is behind it, but there's been an explosion on Ikeda's flagship, and the Kuritans are coming down, screaming for blood. They think the Capellans are to blame, and it looks like we are going to see a good old-fashioned catfight in a minute. Suggestions?"

"I think we need to go with Contingency C," the general said, clearly having gotten the information on the way. "Take the plan right out of their own playbook. We let the two of them fight it out, and then we move in to clean up what's left. Right now it seems they do not blame us, so we get the advantage of being the spectator."

The countess nodded thoughtfully, then glanced over to the screen displaying the Grey Watch commander's face. "Colonel?"

"I say we split the difference," Griffin replied, his eyes smoldering with barely contained excitement. "We were expecting to be outside the city when we activated C, so us already being here gives us the advantage. If we push from the battle line, we can both box the Capellans away from the majority of the residential areas and then have a running start to move deeper into the Capellan-controlled areas of the city. If the rest of the Highlanders and Twelfth Hastati can push them from the south, we might be able to force the battle all the way back to the spaceport."

"I think we can do one better," Maeve interjected, gaining everyone's attention. "We need to keep Stone's Defenders here to make sure this is not a feint to attack the Castle, but we have enough DropShips to move the Sixth Fides and the remains of my personal unit anywhere we need them. Drop us right into the city, and we might be able to grab the HPG right out from under the Capellans' noses as they fight."

The countess considered the thought for a moment. It was certainly a risk, but even Declan saw this was their best chance to retake the HPG compound, and potentially the entire city. The Republic forces had been on the defensive since the arrival of the Kuritan forces, and they had lost their momentum against the Capellans when they did not know what the Kuritans would do, but now the tables had turned.

When it came down to it, it was not as if they had many choices.

Tara's icy blue eyes flickered upward, and this time there was no hesitation in her expression as she looked around the table, her gaze settling on Maeve.

"Do it."

AURORA-CLASS DROPSHIP *FINAL DESTINY*
THE CASTLE
NORTHWIND
REPUBLIC OF THE SPHERE
9 DECEMBER 3150

Declan could not help grinning as he settled into the familiar confines of the command couch of his *Marauder II* and watched the newly repaired panels lighting up. The senior tech had seemed as pleased as Declan was when he informed him that his BattleMech's repairs were finally complete. The techs had worked ceaselessly to get all of the remaining BattleMechs up and running as quickly as possible, and for the coming battle, they could not afford to leave a single ton behind, especially this particular 'Mech.

Declan smiled briefly, thinking of his grandfather's own preferred 'Mech. If you needed heavy, mobile firepower on the battlefield, you could rarely go wrong with a member of the *Marauder* family.

As the 'Mech came to life around him, he glanced out his cockpit at the refitted cargo bay, knowing another assault 'Mech was running preflight checks in the bay to his left, where another special visitor mirrored his own preparations.

Although he could not see her, Lieutenant Colonel Cadha Jaffray was in the cockpit of her 90-ton *Highlander*. The Grey Watch BattleMech, like his own, was equipped with jump jets, and the two of them would help to provide Lady Maeve's forces with some desperately needed firepower. While most of the equipment that the Knight had brought with her was advanced, much of it fit her fighting style: quick, powerful, and deadly. They would do exceptionally well in a city fight, but when it came to going toe-to-toe with what would certainly be the heavy hitters of the Fourth McCarron's Armored Cavalry, they needed all the bruisers they could bring to the party.

The plan was simple. Two *Union* DropShips carrying the Sixth Fides Defenders had already launched for the city, escorted by a pair of *Avengers*. They were meant to split the Capellans' attention by flying east over the city and dropping forces to the southwest of the HPG compound, where they could either link up with the approaching Grey Watch forces or make a quick strike at either the HPG or the spaceport as necessary.

Maeve's DropShip had a different mission. They were going to follow, as if with the same formation, but drop early, between the HPG and the approaching forces. Acting as a heavy recon-in-force, they would help the approaching Grey Watch and Sixth Fides press forward before the Capellans arrived. Besieged by the Kuritans from the north and the Grey Watch and Sixth

Fides from the west, the Capellans would be forced to either make a stand at the HPG or retreat to the spaceport.

Somehow I don't see them retreating just yet, Declan thought.

"Colonel, are you ready?" Maeve's voice rang out over the command channel after having already checked with the rest of her unit. Only a fraction of the BattleMechs she had brought from Terra were aboard the DropShip, one of the only reasons Declan and Jaffray were accompanying them, but all of the others were Republic Armed Forces veterans, hardened in the crucible of battle against the Capellan invaders. The rest of Maeve's unit, which had suffered casualties during the battles on Kearney, had joined the Highlanders to push toward the city.

Jaffray laughed heartily, her joy palpable even through the comm channel. "Are you kidding? I live for this, my lady."

"Lieutenant?"

"Locked and loaded," Declan replied.

"Then we are good to go."

Moments later, Declan felt the rising pressure against his body as the DropShip took to the sky.

THE CASTLE
NORTHWIND
REPUBLIC OF THE SPHERE
9 DECEMBER 3150

The Castle's command center had somehow gotten less crowded but even busier than before. Colonel Alexandre of Stone's Defenders had joined her own troops on the battlements, prepared to counter any strike by opportunistic hostile forces, although the odds of that were low. While Tara Campbell knew the Kuritan commander could have been doing this all for show, his fury had seemed genuine, and if the Kuritans were really coming at the Capellans with all they had, there would be little left for the Republic to finish off afterward.

Still, Tara could not help but press down a thin spike of jealousy. This was the first battle her Highlanders had prepared for on the soil of Northwind where she was unable to serve as she served best, in the cockpit of a 'Mech. While she tried not to think of it being a part of her advancing age, she consoled herself with the acknowledgment that she had a greater role to play. Glancing at General McNamara, she saw an answering flash of understanding: this was another warrior who had suppressed his need to be at the front to ensure that he was able to serve. It might not be what they wanted, but it was what they had.

Turning back to the main screen, Tara raised her voice to be heard over the din. "Please get me a direct feed to Colonel Griffin."

One of the technicians nodded, and the view on the primary screen changed to the interior cockpit camera of the colonel's *Awesome*. Unlike when they had last gone into battle together, this time he went into battle wearing the emblems of the Northwind Highlanders and the Grey Watch. The sight made Tara smile wistfully, and she hoped he knew how much she regretted not being at his side. "How are you holding up, Michael?"

The elder man gave a wry smile. "It's times like these that I almost miss my *Koshi*. I apologize for every time I joked about you being slow to the front, Countess."

Campbell gave him an answering smile, but she felt a twinge of sadness. Not only did she miss wading into battle in her original *Hatchetman*, rather than the *BattleMaster* she now piloted, but she remembered all too well the number-one proponent of a speedy 'Mech: her former aide Tara Bishop, lost long ago in battle with the Jade Falcons. If Tara had been here, no force on the planet would have been able to keep that woman out of a 'Mech.

"Better late than never, Colonel," Tara said.

From the readouts on the command center's screen, the Grey Watch commander was running his *Awesome* full-out, just one step below a sprint. While it had been some time since Tara had traveled the streets of her namesake city, she recognized several landmarks that told her Griffin was nearing the HPG station.

"Any hostiles sighted?" she asked.

"A few brief contacts with some of their tripwire forces, but nothing major yet. I am guessing they are pulling everything back to defend their inner circle."

Tara nodded. With two major hostile units already in the city and a third on the way, the Capellans were likely concentrating their forces as best they could.

"Contact!" The voice came over the speakers in Griffin's neurohelmet, and she recognized Seamus Casey's voice instantly.

From the right, just out of frame, a pair of PPC shots lanced out at the *Tian-Zong* that had just turned the corner. One struck the Capellan's left shoulder, and the other missed cleanly due to the stealth armor the 'Mech was known for.

As Tara observed the battle from different camera feeds, the *Tian-Zong* fired its own primary weapons, a pair of deadly Gauss rifles that flashed silver as they disgorged two watermelon-sized nickel-iron slugs at supersonic speeds. The first round took Griffin's *Awesome* in the left torso, forcing it backward slightly, and the other struck the right leg. The strike seemed to stop the assault 'Mech cold for a moment, and Tara gripped the console in front of her tightly, out of concern for her friend.

She needn't have worried. Griffin's grin was feral as he fired the weapons linked to his primary interlock circuit. She could almost feel the wave of heat from his four particle projection cannons, a tumult of blue-and-white lightning that seemed to strike the *Tian-Zong* everywhere at once.

Facing a minimum of six PPCs between the two Grey Watch BattleMechs, the Capellan MechWarrior chose the better part of valor and ducked down a nearby side street. Griffin held the intersection, waiting for his heat to go down yet ready for another attack, as Seamus ordered the rest of the lance to spread out to regain their forward momentum.

Tara turned back to the general. "How are the Sixth Fides doing?"

"They have begun their drops, but have not yet engaged," McNamara replied. "The Kuritans have just blown past them. The Sixth are under orders not to fire first, and apparently the Kuritans feel the same."

Tara pursed her lips into a tight line, but she was not surprised. Hoping she could goad some of the Kuritans into breaking away from the main force had been a long shot, but the last thing she wanted to do was to divert their berserker charge toward her forces. The Sixth Fides were exceptional warriors, but even they could not take on two full regiments of Kuritan warriors by themselves, and the rest of Tara's forces were not in position yet.

"ETA for Lady Maeve?"

"Nine minutes."

Glancing over at the screen, which showed Griffin moving again, Tara estimated his troops would be in position within five.

The room fell silent, everyone's eyes glued to the screens as a line of black Kuritan 'Mechs with crimson trim flashed past one of Tara's picket forces like a stampede. She gestured to highlight the screen and witnessed dozens of Draconis 'Mechs surge past an old Grey Watch *Wasp* that had been tasked with providing reconnaissance.

A Capellan *Lao Hu* stepped out from a side street in ambush, in the same way the *Tian-Zong* had attacked Colonel Griffin, but it fared even worse. Every Kuritan in range lit off its full weapons array, and the heavy BattleMech was struck with a deafening wave of directed energy, missiles, and autocannon shells. One moment the pristine 'Mech was standing, and a moment later it was slumped against the wall of a brick building, its left leg, left arm, and head completely missing, along with several meters of the building itself.

The command center quieted at the sudden brutality of it all, and even Tara felt herself straighten, shocked by the Kuritan forces not even bothering to slow down.

The timer on the wall flashed, showing the countdown until Lady Maeve's DropShip arrived at its destination, and the balloon truly went up.

Four minutes.

"All right, people. Let's be about it."

CHAPTER 13

"All problems, personal, national, or combat, become smaller if you don't dodge them, but confront them. Touch a thistle timidly, and it pricks you; grasp it boldly, and its spines crumble."

—William Halsey

HPG COMPOUND
TARA, NORTHWIND
REPUBLIC OF THE SPHERE
9 DECEMBER 3150

Sang-shao Lindsey Baxter tightened her hands on the controls of her *Pillager* and stepped up to the inner defensive line she had prepared for just this sort of eventuality. Despite knowing she should still be in the command center and trying to figure out what had gone so terribly wrong, she couldn't be happier to be in the cockpit. She had justified the necessity by saying that the *gao-shiao-zhang*'s absence on the field necessitated her presence, but even the unique interpretation of her orders that the new Warrior House Imarra's new commander had taken did not truly justify her taking the field.

When she had heard of the Warrior House's strike on Tara's residential district, she had tried to keep her temper, knowing Imarra's traditional autonomy would protect *Shiao-zhang* Garzon from any negative repercussions over his creative interpretation of his orders, but she still wanted to know why the man had chosen such a reckless course. While it was probably inevitable that the Republic forces would take advantage of the Kuritans' rapid change of allegiance, the damage to the city and its people had only heightened the sheer focused intensity of the Highlanders' advance.

Before departing for the 'Mech bay, Lindsey had seen battleROM footage from a House Imarra *Raven* of a Grey Watch *UrbanMech*, the slow, lumbering machine leading a lance of its brethren down one of the side streets. The sight of the four 'Mechs, hardly impressive at the best of times, was terrifying now, their purpose clear in their gait, the flames of the city burning behind them and throwing the scene into a brutal tableau of flickering shadows.

It didn't help when the four *UrbanMech*s fired their autocannons nearly in unison, and blasted one of the legs right off the *Raven*.

Three of the Grey Watch BattleMechs did not even slow down and just walked past the struggling Capellan 'Mech contemptuously. The fourth, likely the lance leader, peered down at the damaged House Imarra 'Mech like it were a wounded bird, and angled the weapons on its two stubby arms carefully—

The video feed abruptly cut off. Lindsey desperately hoped the *Raven* pilot had punched out...

Focusing back on the immediate threat, she heard the first calls of contact, and her front rank of warriors began firing. She switched to the general channel and heard the carefully measured updates from her advance units. Posted nearly six blocks ahead, they had been painstakingly pre-positioned to take advantage of the inner defensive redoubts her troops had been cultivating since originally taking the city. While her regiment would never have the intimate knowledge of the city the Northwind natives had, she had been very proud of her officers for building a careful, layered defense that could hold back most attackers.

What they could not have anticipated, however, was the sheer, mindless ferocity of the Kuritan forces. Having plotted their defensive positions for days, her troops had prepared for the onslaught, knowing exactly which weapons would be in range when and how best to use them, along with the plentiful cover, to their advantage.

As the Kuritans approached, Capellan extended-range PPC fire, long-range missiles, Gauss rounds, and light-caliber autocannons stabbed out at the first line of incoming BattleMechs, inflicting hellacious damage. She saw a *Jenner* go down under a hail of fire, but another quickly passed it, eager to get into range. This second *Jenner* attempted to get closer, not even bothering to fire its weapons at extreme range, only for the Capellans' fire to take it down next.

Unfortunately, that allowed a pair of *Panther*s, running all out, to reach firing range. Their PPCs fired almost as one, and one stream of man-made lightning clipped the side of a building while the second struck a *Tian-Zong* in the middle rank.

More Kuritan BattleMechs swarmed forward, and Lindsey realized they were not going to stop. The Combine warriors were in full berserker mode, heedless of the damage they would sustain to get themselves in range, willing to accept any losses to address the wrongs that had allegedly been committed against them.

Her first realization was quickly followed by a second, more terrible one: she could not win this battle with just her own regiment. House Imarra's forces were still pulling back to the compound, and Laurel's Legion was still trailing the Kuritans. The Draconis Combine troops would take hideous amounts of damage, especially when Laurel's Legion struck them from behind, but she could not keep her own regiment intact or hold the HPG compound if things continued in this fashion.

A fact confirmed as the first rumblings from the approaching DropShips hit her ears.

They came from the west, having swung around the outskirts of the city, and she saw their deployment hatches were already open. Some of her 'Mechs aimed skyward and fired at the hovering DropShips, only to receive a withering barrage of fire in reply. Torn between the Combine 'Mechs on the ground and the hovering DropShips, her regiment had few good options.

Switching to transmit, Lindsey relayed new orders to her command. "All Fourth MAC forces, prepare for Contingency Eta-Two!"

There was a noticeable pause, and then her battalion commanders confirmed the order, although she heard the hesitation in their voices. Eta-2 was one of several contingency plans that involved a clear and present threat to their hold on the HPG compound. It called for an orderly withdrawal to the secondary defensive lines, while leaving behind some surprises to slow down their enemies.

With a deft flick of a switch, she brought up a private channel to Qiao. "Julie, I need some assistance."

"What do you need?" the other commander responded. "We are twelve minutes out."

"We are going to Eta-Two and are falling back to the secondary defensive positions. Can you swing around and provide us some cover without risking your main force?"

To her credit, Qiao did not hesitate. "We will give you the out you need. What do you want us to do from there?"

"Slip through the south corridor once we are free. We're going to inflict maximum damage on the enemy, but we can't afford to be held up here."

Ikeda swore lightly, careful not to trigger the microphone in his neurohelmet as he fired another stream of explosive shells at a Capellan 'Mech blocking his clear run down the city streets. His 85-ton *Tai-sho* stomped down the avenue as the smaller Capellan BattleMechs rapidly adjusted their positioning before him.

Apparently the Capellan commander had realized her stopgap maneuver would not work, that his valiant warriors possessed enough momentum, firepower, and rage to burst through the walls of deadly fire she had set up.

"All forces, press forward, maximum speed!" he commanded. "Let none of these dishonorable curs escape our wrath!"

Already prepared for the order, his recon and pursuit forces shot ahead and unflinchingly faced the withering fire as only true warriors of the Dragon could.

Suddenly, one of his subordinates came over his comms with an update: "*Sho-sho*, we have Capellan forces attacking us from the rear!"

Ikeda smiled grimly, seeing the maneuver for the desperation it was. The Capellan regiment known as Laurel's Legion had been following his forces for some time now, careful not to engage, but it was clear they had been ordered to distract him.

"Rear guard," he transmitted, "engage at will, but maintain your forward momentum. Fourth Dieron, turn and engage the Capellan harassers!"

It was clear what *Sang-shao* Baxter was trying to do: she had finally realized her perfidy would gain her nothing against elite Kuritan warriors, and she sought to flee from what she had wrought.

She would not succeed.

Even if her distraction had been effective, Ikeda's rear guard comprised some of his heaviest BattleMechs, their speed limited by the armor and weaponry they carried. It was a valiant effort to try distracting him, but it would come to naught, and he intended to exact a high price for their betrayal.

Ikeda focused on the battle ahead of him, however. His jaw clenched as a company of Fourth McCarron's Armored Cavalry 'Mechs took cover behind a line of buildings and popped out at random intervals to fire down the tight confines of the streets. Unlike the earlier encounters, the Capellans were not even trying to hide their numbers, seemingly content to use cover as protection rather than for deception...or so it seemed.

He spotted movement down the street and switched to a direct line to his scout lance. "Show me what the enemy is doing now!"

A *Jenner* took to the air on jets of plasma, barely dodging the sparkling brilliance of lasers and autocannon-tracer fire that lit up the sky. In mid-jump, the *Jenner* cut the power to its jets and dropped like a stone, then bent its knees to take the impact from the sudden descent. "*Sho-sho*, the main body of the Capellan forces are pulling back from the front line!"

Ikeda instantly saw what his foes were trying to accomplish. They were sacrificing one of their companies to keep his forces from catching up to them, forfeiting their own lives to ensure that his Hikage could not meet them decisively in battle, much like Baxter had attempted with the strike by Laurel's Legion.

Are there no depths to which these Capellans will sink? How does the Coordinator believe these are worthy allies for the Combine?

Switching to his command channel, he ordered his vanguard elements to give chase. "Katana Company, press through! The rest of us will follow at speed!"

Katana Company, his heavy-attack force composed of his largest 'Mechs, pushed forward at his order, shielding their lighter counterparts as they charged through into the intersection. Ikeda's command company followed. Unlike his recon elements, Katana Company's heavy BattleMechs had both the armor and weapons to confront the Capellan rear guard head-on, and he intended to stop for nothing.

Spotting a Capellan *Emperor*, he triggered one of his extended-range PPCs, sending a cerulean lance of charged particles at the large 'Mech. To his surprise, the assault 'Mech nimbly slipped to one side, the shot missing it by meters. For a moment, he thought it was going to return fire, but it stepped down a side alley, quickly breaking line of sight.

The casual way the Capellan 'Mech had disengaged sent a wave of heat through him, and he pressed forward into the fray.

As he'd feared, the Capellans had been hellishly effective at slowing his assault. Nearly a full lance of enemy 'Mechs were down, but their metal corpses were piling up on the street, blocking the easiest routes for his BattleMechs. Some of his jump-capable 'Mechs were leapfrogging over the obstructions, but the steady hail of fire from the remaining Capellan forces made it slow going.

Pulling back one of his 'Mech's legs, Ikeda kicked over the fallen remains of a Capellan *Duan Gung*, and pressed farther into the intersection. A *Cataphract* stepped up into the breach ahead of him, its autocannon chattering, and the shells cut an ugly swath of damage across his *Tai-sho*'s chest.

Ikeda shifted his crosshairs onto the centerline of the Capellan heavy 'Mech and riposted with his own autocannon. The Ultra-class autocannon's fusillade ripped into the *Cataphract*'s chest, and the whole 'Mech shivered as the slugs burrowed deep enough to clip the massive gyroscope that helped the 'Mech maintain its balance. The *Cataphract* raised its other arm, but Ikeda was an instant quicker on the trigger. He fired one of his PPCs again, but this time, the particle projection cannon hit right on target, spearing into the *Cataphract*'s chest to capitalize on the damage from his autocannon. The flickering bluish-white lightning carved through the remains of the 'Mech's emerald-green armor, leaving long black streaks of charred steel as it cut its way inside. The entire BattleMech slumped over, the delicate balance imparted by the gyro now lost, and it collapsed to the ground.

Refocusing on the larger battle, Ikeda's grim expression turned into a fierce grin as his forces reorganized and rushed down the now-cleared alleys. As he advanced, a *Rokurokubi* piloted by one of his lance commanders dashed down a side street, its legs pistoning into a sprint to chase after the slower Capellan BattleMechs as they retreated. Turning back to the rest of his force, Ikeda ordered the others to follow, allowing the lance commander their rightful place as being the first off the mark.

Until the *Rokurokubi* reached the nearby intersection, where a brilliant explosion blew the 'Mech's leg clean off.

Vibramines.

This time, Ikeda did not care who heard him swear.

CHAPTER 14

"They did WHAT?"

—Countess Tara Campbell, 9 December 3150

AURORA-CLASS DROPSHIP *FINAL DESTINY*
NORTHWIND
REPUBLIC OF THE SPHERE
9 DECEMBER 3150

Declan's head snapped up as he heard Maeve swear. As he could not see her in the cockpit of her *Tundra Wolf*, he switched over to her private channel. "Problems?"

He could almost hear her nod. "I just got word from the Sixth Fides' DropShips: the Fourth MAC has pulled back from their forward defensive positions."

"Shouldn't that be a good thing?" Jaffray's voice cut in over the line. "The Kuritans must have hit them even harder than we had hoped."

"Not hard enough," the Knight replied. "They withdrew in good order, and now they look like they are going to make a stand at the HPG compound."

Declan fought down his own desire to swear. The plan had been simple. While the Kuritans and Capellans fought each other, the Grey Watch was to advance from the west, focusing on the Capellans and opening a new front in the conflict. That was when the Capellans were supposed to break and retreat toward the HPG, only to find that the Sixth Fides had dropped in behind them. That would have put the Capellans between the Grey Watch hammer and the Fides anvil and force them to abandon the compound. Then, the Grey Watch and Sixth Fides would link up and divert the Capellans' retreat toward their DropShips at the spaceport. With a little luck, the Capellans and Kuritans would have their last stand there, where they would do little damage to the city, and the Republic forces would be able to deal with whoever was left standing. At that point, hopefully whoever that was would be in the mood to talk, since they likely would not be strong enough to take on the relatively fresh Republic forces.

Unfortunately, all of that relied on the Sixth Fides landing and maneuvering in time to prevent the Fourth MAC from taking defensive positions in the HPG compound. If the Capellans had already abandoned their forward positions...

"How close is the Grey Watch?" Declan asked. *If they could move forward fast enough, give the Sixth Fides time to disembark...*

The hesitation in Maeve's voice told him everything he needed to know. "Not close enough."

Declan pulled up sensor feeds on his secondary monitor. A single glance confirmed that the Grey Watch was still nearly fifteen minutes away from the planned rendezvous, and the Fourth MAC would pass through the same space in less than ten. If the Sixth Fides were not in place by then, the Highlanders would either have to let the Capellans reinforce the HPG compound or risk being caught between the fleeing Capellans and the rapidly approaching Kuritans.

"Can we set a new rendezvous?" MechWarrior Stephens, the remaining member of Maeve's original lance, chimed in.

"We'll have to set a point on the far side of the compound," Maeve replied. "It'll take us a little longer to get into position, but we should be able to strike the rear entrance to try forcing a breach. We can hopefully slow their entry, which should help to keep them off balance."

Declan stayed silent, thinking of all the things that could go wrong. The Republic troops outside the compound would be conducting a siege while the Kuritans would attempt to do the same thing on the opposite side. While the two forces would eventually breach the compound's exterior walls, they would be facing relatively fresh Capellans inside, while other Capellan units could very well be surrounding them. The Capellans would have to decide which thrust was the greater threat, but there was a fifty-fifty chance of devastating losses for the Republic.

That was assuming, of course, the Kuritans did not change sides again, and strike at the Republic while there was an opportunity to have their cake and eat it too.

"What's our ETA to the rendezvous point?" he asked, the first elements of a new plan forming in his head.

"Two minutes."

"And to the compound?"

"Four minutes," Maeve replied, her voice suspicious.

Jaffray laughed. "Oh, I see where this is going. You truly are a Highlander, lad..."

Lindsey Baxter ran her *Pillager* through the gap in the defensive barricades, and turned to prepare for the Kuritans' arrival. She needn't have bothered: as soon as she was through, several other 'Mechs stepped into the gap, protecting their commander and sealing off the block.

Now that she had a moment to breathe, she switched over to Qiao's private channel. "Julie, how are you holding up?"

"No issues," Qiao replied, although Lindsey could hear the sounds of the *sang-shao*'s *Emperor* running full out. "Your rear guard and the minefield gave us the head start we needed." Her voice grew more solemn. "I have a couple of Maxim transports shadowing the area... When the Kuritans have passed, they will attempt search and recovery."

Lindsey had known from the beginning that using this particular contingency plan would cost the lives of whichever unit she left behind to delay the Kuritan forces, but she appreciated her friend trying to help any survivors. "What is your location?"

"My lead elements have just reached the rendezvous point, and we are preparing to move to the next phase on your command."

Lindsey smiled thinly, as the situation was finally going their way. She and the commander of Laurel's Legion had worked on the contingency planning at great length, and they had been prepared for the possibility that they might need to abandon the forward defensive perimeter.

The rendezvous point to the east had easy access to the most likely routes an attacker would take toward the compound, as well as a secured route to the compound itself. Depending on what the Kuritans did, the Legion could strike them from an unexpected direction or do an end run to support the Fourth MAC from the compound.

"Hold position," Lindsey replied, "but prepared for a direct counterattack. We don't know for sure that you were able to shake them."

Qiao laughed, a surprising, unexpected sound. "Lindsey, I don't think I shook them at all, they are far too focused on the prize... Trust me, they are coming for you."

Lindsey was about to respond when the first calls of "Contact!" came over the main channel. A quick glance showed her front ranks of BattleMechs firing from their defensive positions, and she quickly switched her channel to Colonel Tompkins-Centrella, who had taken command of the HPG compound's interior defenses. While the Canopian commander's remaining light elements were providing firsthand intelligence of the approaching Kuritan and Republic forces, her remaining command elements were positioned on the compound's walls, for additional fire support. "Status report, Colonel."

"We are attacking enemy units as they come into view. We can open the inner courtyard upon your—" The colonel's voice froze for a moment. "DropShip incoming!"

Baxter's eyes darted upward, where she saw a single Republic DropShip roaring forward on approach, its cargo bay doors gaping open.

"Go, go, go!"

Declan heard the dropmaster's signal and immediately stepped his *Marauder II* out into the air. The *Final Destiny*'s cargo doors were already open, and the four teams of Sixth Fides Nighthawk Mk. XXX power armor had already taken to the sky to descend into the HPG compound and secure it. Declan had watched most of them land safely, although one had landed on the catwalk below the HPG dish and slipped off the icy surface.

The effect was surreal—leaping out into sky a hundred meters from the ground, the hovering DropShip alight with energy as its main weapons fired at any Capellan forces in range. The Capellans had believed themselves safe within their defenses, but Declan watched a Canopian *Eyleuka* on the wall of the compound take a strike from one of the *Final Destiny*'s laser turrets, forcing it to stumble backward and tumble off the wall.

He did not have the opportunity to see what happened next, as he was concentrating on hitting his jump jets to slow the decent of his 100-ton 'Mech. On his secondary monitor, he saw Maeve's *Tundra Wolf* dropping down beside him, with Stephens' *Peacekeeper* jumping a moment later. Declan and Maeve landed first, and the two lanced out with their weaponry. Declan skewered a *Victor* in the back with his paired PPCs, and Maeve struck one of the Minion hovertanks with her medium lasers.

There was no sign of Lieutenant Colonel Jaffray.

Maeve clearly noticed the same thing. "Colonel, are you all right?"

"Certainly," came Jaffray's far-too-calm voice. "One moment."

Although he knew he should remain focused, Declan looked up to see her *Highlander* still poised on the end of the drop ramp, waiting patiently, making no move to descend. Then the DropShip banked to the east, and she stepped out into the air.

The movement of the DropShip gave her a bit of sideways motion, and her immense assault Mech descended quickly, banking toward the wall of the compound.

Laser and tracer fire sliced through the air on either side of the *Highlander*, but it seemed completely oblivious to the threat. It came down quickly, almost too quickly, and Declan knew the 'Mech was going to miss the wall, coming down on the wrong side—deep in the midst of the Capellan forces...

At the last moment, Jaffray ignited her jump jets at full power, cleared the wall, and landed atop the *Eyleuka* with both feet. The turning Canopian 'Mech had no chance to regain its balance, taking the full brunt of the *Highlander*'s 90 tons directly on its right arm. The already-unbalanced BattleMech fell backward and crashed to the ground two stories below, unmoving.

Balancing carefully on the 'Mech-scale catwalk the *Eyleuka* had just vacated, Jaffray whirled to face off against the *Victor* Declan had attacked. The *Victor*'s burst of heavy-autocannon fire carved a vicious gash just above Jaffray's left hip, and then a quartet of SRMs, fired almost as an afterthought, sent a series of small explosions across the *Highlander*'s chest.

If her descent from the departing DropShip or artful landing had unbalanced the Grey Watch warrior, there was no sign of it. She fired her *Highlander*'s medium lasers and Gauss rifle at the *Victor*, the well-aimed strikes taking her opponent in the torso.

Declan moved to assist her, but his 'Mech shook slightly as the second Minion fired its medium pulse lasers at him, scoring damage on his right arm. Declan replied with his own medium lasers and triggered a Gauss rifle round that ripped the glacis armor off the front of the hovertank. Having dealt with the Minion, he saw Stephens put a pair of PPC bolts into the downed *Eyleuka*.

Maeve's voice came over the command channel, quickly. "Stephens, hold the gate! Declan, you and I are going up on the battlements!"

She did not wait for a response before hitting her jump jets and launching into the sky.

As the Republic 'Mechs began to drop, Lindsey was already in motion, rushing her *Pillager* around the corner, her voice strained. "Open the gates!"

Unfortunately, the compound's reinforced walls were thick, and the armored gates remained stubbornly closed. Whether the enemy was jamming her communications or already had people inside, she was not going to get much help from there.

For the briefest of moments, she considered ordering some of her jump-capable BattleMechs back into the compound, but she was hesitant to have her MechWarriors leap over the wall blindly. She had seen several battle armor squads and at least one heavy 'Mech lance drop into the compound, which was a fairly sizeable force for the limited space. She could send a number of lighter 'Mechs in, but they would be at a considerable weight disadvantage, and she could not spare the heavier 'Mechs her regiment would need to hold off the approaching Kuritan forces.

She shook her head. *For now, the Republic can have the compound. When we triumph, I will drag them out of there myself.*

And if we lose, it will not matter.

"Hold to the walls!" she ordered. "Prepare for the incoming Kuritan forces!"

Her 'Mechs stood alongside her, with their backs literally to the compound's armored walls. This HPG, one of the few working specimens left in the Inner Sphere, had brought her to this planet, and she refused to give it up for long. If Ikeda wanted this precious prize, he would have to take it from her.

In the distance, the first Kuritan 'Mechs appeared, spilling out from the darkness like a crimson wave, and she gave the order to open fire.

CHAPTER 15

"All Grey Watch forces, forward at full speed. Cadha has changed the tune on us, and I refuse to be late to the dance."

—Colonel Michael Griffin, 9 December 3150

HPG COMPOUND
TARA, NORTHWIND
REPUBLIC OF THE SPHERE
9 DECEMBER 3150

Lindsey Baxter's forces continue to engage the approaching Kuritans. While the Hikage advanced with the same merciless intensity as before, she sensed a hesitation in their actions: they had no way of knowing if she had mined the streets between them, and they were cautious of losing more of their numbers to the same trick. Since she had consolidated her forces into a smaller area, the Kuritans were taking brutal damage as they approached, although they gave back nearly as good as they got.

Unfortunately, her enemies were destined to be disappointed for their caution: she had not mined the area. Instead, she had counted on her 'Mechs atop the compound's walls to do that for her, using Thunder missiles to scatter FASCAM mines. However, with Republic 'Mechs actually inside the compound now, she needed to husband her remaining Thunder missiles until she desperately needed them.

Turning back to the battle ahead, she called out orders as the Kuritans passed the designated mark. "Forward rank, move and fire!"

The first row of her heavy hitters advanced into the intersection and loosed their entire complement of fire in a devastating alpha strike before slipping behind a new building to cool down.

A Kuritan *Dragon* took a withering flurry of fire from a Fourth MAC *Helios*, the heavy 'Mech shattering armor with its "Emperor Bones" Gauss rifle, and following up with a flurry of medium lasers and short-range missiles. One of the lasers missed, but the *Dragon* weathered the rest of the fire like it had taken a blast from a shotgun, freezing in place for an instant—just long enough for the *Helios'* lancemate, a heavy *Jinggau*, to add its Gauss rifle and medium laser battery to the fray.

The *Jinggau's* weaponry cut away the lower half of the *Dragon's* right arm, pockmarked the torso, and ripped the left leg off completely. She heard a ragged cheer from some of her troops as the *Dragon* went down, but a *Naginata* took its place up the middle of the street, sending a cloud of nearly four dozen long-range missiles into the air. The *Jinggau* tried to avoid the missile swarm, but more than a dozen warheads detonated across its armor before it got clear.

And still the Kuritans were closing.

"Second rank, engage!"

The next wave of Lindsey's 'Mechs sidestepped into the road again, their weapons firing, the glare of energy weapons and the report of autocannons echoing in the tight confines of the city.

Unfortunately, this time the Kuritans were prepared, and they were already firing. A pair of extended-range large lasers tore away one of the *Helios'* shoulder-mounted SRM launchers, and the 'Mech barely made it back into cover before a PPC blasted apart the building it had been standing in front of.

Her forces were moving to new defensive positions, but there was nowhere else to go. The fight was devolving into a brawl, and even Lindsey found herself dragged in as a pair of Kuritan 'Mechs, a *Shugenja* and an *Avalanche*, stepped into the thoroughfare she was guarding.

Realizing she was outgunned, she cut sharply to the right and lunged at the *Shugenja*, careful to keep the buildings at her back. She knew she needed to take on the heaviest threat first, and the armament that the *Shugenja* carried could easily ruin her day. As she advanced, it fired its medium-range missile rack, sending a torrent of dead-fire missiles at her, and followed up with its arm-mounted large lasers. Both lasers bored into her *Pillager's* arm, pushing the wireframe diagnostic into a harsh amber, but she managed to raise both arms and let fly with her paired Gauss rifles.

The pair of nickel-iron slugs plowed straight through the *Shugenja's* arm and tore the two lasers off. The large 'Mech overcompensated for the loss of its limb, scraping the other arm against a nearby building.

In an instant, Lindsey had the advantage. Now that her opponent's large lasers were gone, she charged forward and smashed her 'Mech into the *Shugenja*, sending it toppling to the ground.

The *Avalanche* moved in quickly to support its lancemate, skewering her with its quartet of extended-range medium lasers and cutting away shards of torso armor near her right arm.

She gave a feral grin as she felt the new rounds snap into the breeches of her Gauss rifles, and once again sent them downrange.

The devastation was worse for the smaller 'Mech. Despite the *Avalanche's* speed and relatively undamaged armor, the two Gauss slugs struck the 'Mech like paired sledgehammers. The *Avalanche* stumbled backward and slumped against a wall, a massive hole in the center of its chest where its gyro should be.

Lindsey whirled around, seeking out another target, and took a shot of opportunity down the street at a heavy Kuritan 'Mech she did not stop to identify. Her large laser dealt a glancing blow, and the 'Mech was gone.

She spared a glance at her secondary screen and saw that her forces were fully engaged. *Too fully engaged*, she thought. She couldn't afford to be bogged down here, especially with the Draconis troops still relatively fresh. While her regiment had whittled down the Kuritans' numbers so far, she had no doubt there were still too many of them.

But her monitors told her everything she needed to know: with Republic forces currently inside the compound, she needed to pull back to regroup. While she had never seriously expected this situation to occur, she had drafted a set of contingency plans that had them falling back to Kohler Spaceport, where their parked DropShips could provide additional long-distance firepower to dissuade the Kuritans from following them. It was the last sort of plan she would have recommended, but even the Kuritans would hesitate to run into the teeth of nearly four Capellan regiments with artillery and long-range fire support.

"All units, prepare to move to Contingency Foxtrot Zulu," she commanded, then switched her comm channel back to Qiao. "Julie, can you provide us with some support again?"

"Affirmative," Qiao replied. "Pick the location, and we will break you free—"

Another voice cut into the command channel. "Imarra actual to MAC actual, we have an emergency."

Garzon.

"What is it, *Shiao-zhang*?"

"We are heavily engaged, and unable to secure the route to the spaceport. We have multiple enemy forces pressing us."

She glanced at her secondary screen, desperately trying to find out how the Kuritans had somehow got between her and her escape route without her knowing.

"Please confirm, Imarra Actual," she replied. "You have Combine forces engaging you?"

This time, the signal was a bit stronger, allowing his voice to be heard more clearly over the comms. "Negative, *Sang-shao*. We have Republic forces engaged, confirming Highlander Grey Watch."

Lindsey swore vehemently as she saw what had happened, not caring if the other commanders heard her. Instead of diving into battle and taking advantage of her preoccupation to cause further damage, the Grey Watch had slipped around the rear of the HPG compound, knowing that if the fighting got too hot, she would probably order a retreat to her DropShips. By striking at House Imarra, the unit holding open the back door for her regiment, the Grey Watch cut off her main avenue of retreat while also exacting a little payback for Warrior House Imarra's earlier strike at the residential zone.

She quickly switched her comms over to include *Sang-shao* Qiao. "Julie! Change of plans. Cut through the south side of the city and support Warrior

House Imarra. Unless I'm wrong, we are going to have more company very soon, and we'll need to reorganize quickly."

"What about you?" Qiao asked, also seeing the tactical dilemma. Without Laurel's Legion to help them disengage, the Fourth MAC was going to be fighting for every centimeter of their withdrawal, and Lindsey was going to lose a lot of her troops.

Garzon must have thought the same thing. "*Sang-shao*," he said, "we can take on the Grey Watch without assistance—"

"Negative, *Shiao-zhang*," Lindsey replied harshly, too frustrated to worry about Garzon's feelings at this point. "I expect to be pressed hard once the rest of the Highlanders arrive. If they are not working with the Kuritans, we will likely have a three-way battle on our hands very soon. But if the Highlanders *are* working with the Kuritans, I expect them to send their second battalion right on your heels, to cut off our escape. If we do not get clear soon, none of this is going to matter."

Julie would not let the situation go, however. "What about you?"

"I will make my own opening." Lindsey switched over to her command company's channel. "This is Fourth MAC Actual. All jump-capable units, I want you inside that compound yesterday. All other units..." Her gaze flickered to the compound's reinforced gate, still stubbornly closed against all comers. She raised her weapons and locked her lasers and PPC on a new target.

"Bring down that gate!"

CHAPTER 16

Old men forget; yet all shall be forgot,
But he'll remember, with advantages,
What feats he did that day.

—William Shakespeare, *Henry V*, Act 4, Scene III

HPG COMPOUND
TARA, NORTHWIND
REPUBLIC OF THE SPHERE
9 DECEMBER 3150

The first realization that they were in serious trouble came when Declan looked down from his position atop one of the HPG compound's walls and saw an entire company of Capellan BattleMechs turn toward the gate and open fire.

Leveling his arm-mounted weapons, he aimed at the nearest 'Mech, a *Tian-Zong*, and fired both PPCs, followed by a slug from his Gauss rifle. His target took the shots in its heavily armored torso and arm, but the Capellan sent back two gleaming Gauss slugs of its own; one struck his *Marauder II* in the shoulder, and the other spent itself on the wall. As Declan prepared for another salvo, he saw two 'Mechs take to the sky, intending to land inside the compound and split their focus.

"We have incoming!" he warned, struggling to keep his focus on the earthbound 'Mechs. If he could keep sniping at them, he could prevent them from getting too close and causing trouble.

"Understood," Maeve replied, her voice cutting through the chatter of weapons fire. "Stephens, be ready to hold the door! I've got this." Before Declan could say anything, she jumped her *Tundra Wolf* in a low arc back into the compound.

For a moment, he was tempted to argue with her, but her maneuver had been the most tactically sound option they had available at the moment. Her weapons had no minimum-range limitations and could handle a variety of ranges, while his were ideal for distant targets.

Atop one of the other walls, Lieutenant Colonel Cadha Jaffray's *Highlander* was still firing; her Gauss rifle and missiles lanced out at the *Tian-Zong* and increased the already significant damage Declan had inflicted, causing it to drop to one knee. A second strike from her missile rack struck one of the Capellan 'Mech's Gauss rifles, causing it to explode with a burst of hellish energy, nearly toppling the 'Mech. Out of sheer frustration Declan added another PPC shot into the mix, but it missed cleanly.

The first of the jumping Capellan 'Mechs, a *Vindicator*, landed directly in front of Stephens' *Peacekeeper*. Maeve's lancemate let loose with an alpha strike that shook the enemy BattleMech to the core—a flurry of PPCs, a large laser, a plasma rifle, and short-range missiles. Declan winced in sympathy for the Republic pilot, as the heat buildup from the attack must have been agonizing.

Stephens' PPCs carved huge divots out of the *Vindicator*, and the laser sliced an ugly weal across the 'Mech's ribs. The plasma rifle did the most damage, however, imparting further heat to its target, making the Capellan MechWarrior more hesitant to use their energy weapons to strike back, worried it would cause the 'Mech's fusion engine to shut down from overheating.

The pilot should not have worried, as Jaffray's *Highlander* lowered one arm in the *Vindicator*'s direction and launched a salvo of short-range missiles from one gauntleted fist. The missiles capitalized on the earlier damage and dropped the lighter 'Mech to the ground.

The other Capellan that had leaped the compound wall was a 60-ton *Ti Ts'ang*. Lacking the heat worries of its companion, the 'Mech fired a torrent of energy from its battery of medium and small lasers, sending a riot of color at Maeve's *Tundra Wolf*. Her 'Mech weathered the storm bravely for a moment, and then lashed out with her own lasers, carving angry streaks across the Capellan's armor.

Not seeking to be outdone, the *Ti Ts'ang* raised the double-bladed battle-ax in its right hand. Maeve backpedaled, continuing to fire ineffectual medium lasers into her opponent's chest. Before Declan could respond, the Knight lit off her extended-range PPCs and hammered the *Ti Ts'ang* in the arm, charring and scoring the armor over the hand gripping the ax.

The Capellan MechWarrior was unfazed, however, and still brought the battle-ax down. Its depleted-uranium blade slashed the wrist of Maeve's 'Mech, and sparks flew from severed control runs.

Declan swiveled his torso to get the *Ti Ts'ang* under his guns, but he needn't have worried. Maeve was an experienced MechWarrior, and knew how to react to such an attack. Instead of backpedaling out of range of her opponent's weapons, she raised her arm right over the *Ti Ts'ang*'s wrist and triggered all of her medium lasers. The rush of heat must have soared within her cockpit, but the reaction was instantaneous: the laser energy ate through the Capellan 'Mech's wrist, and the battle-ax dropped at her feet.

For the briefest of moments, Declan imagined the Capellan MechWarrior was incredibly lucky that Maeve's *Tundra Wolf* lacked hand actuators to pick up the fallen ax, but he quickly saw she was no slouch at close-quarters combat. A single kick of her 'Mech's massive feet destabilized the *Ti Ts'ang*, and her next salvo knocked it to the ground.

"Incoming!" Jaffray shouted.

The warning came just in time, and Declan swiveled back to see another 'Mech take to the air, a Capellan *Wasp*. It barely made it off the ground, as Declan's PPCs and Gauss rifle struck a moment after Jaffray's missiles. What little remained of the 20-ton 'Mech collapsed to the ground, succumbing to gravity's call.

Declan realized they were losing the battle to keep the Capellans out of the compound. Every jumping 'Mech forced them to split their focus, and they all had to be running low on expendable munitions. He had been husbanding the last of his Gauss rifle rounds, and Colonel Jaffray had to be in a very similar place. Maeve and Stephens had a greater number of energy weapons, but their magazines running low still put them at a tactical disadvantage.

Also, every jumping BattleMech they dealt with allowed the other Capellan 'Mechs to keep firing their own weapons at the gate. The gate's reinforced armor was already pockmarked and starting to buckle, and he knew they had little time left to deal with the situation before the door would fail and an entire company of angry Capellans would flood the compound.

"Watch Five ta Knight Lance, what is yer status?" Seamus' voice came over the comm, indicating that he must be nearby.

Jaffray responded first. "Major, we are under heavy attack from the Fourth MAC. Can I assume you have something to do with that? We're being jammed."

Declan glanced at his communications display and realized she was right. Aside from the four of them, he was no longer getting the tactical updates he had been receiving earlier. He spotted a Capellan *Raven* rushing down one of the nearby streets, and snap-shot a PPC to try to tag it. The bolt of cerulean lightning missed, but the *Raven* did not wait around for him to try again, quickly disappearing down a side street.

"Ye could say that," Seamus replied. "The Sixth Fides troops ye couldnae take with ye managed ta find a landing zone and caught up with us, and we are pressing the Imarra forces hard. The colonel thinks we are content to keep them from linking up, but we are pressing forward in yer direction. Do ye need assistance?"

"Yes!" Declan replied at the same time that Jaffray responded, "No."

"Major," Jaffray said as if Declan had not spoken, "we are going to hold this compound for as long as we can, but I am assuming the rest of the Highlanders are about to dive into the fray. We need you to keep House Imarra from reinforcing the Fourth for as long as you can."

"Confirmed, Colonel." Seamus responded, his tone carefully measured.

A moment later, Declan was unsurprised to see a light flash on his private channel.

"How ye holding up, lad?" Seamus asked.

"Just fine," Declan replied, firing off another one-two punch from his PPCs as a *Duan Gung* began shooting up at the 'Mechs on the wall.

"Ye just need to hold on for a little longer, Dec," his grandfather said. "The rest of the Highlanders will be there in a few minutes."

"We'll hold," Declan said, although he sensed Seamus knew exactly what he was thinking. *They* would hold, all right, but the gate would not. Not only that, but if the Highlanders had entered the city on a straight-line course from the Castle, they would have to fight their way through the Kuritan forces as well as the Capellans, which would take even more time. Either way, it looked like they were going to be in the middle of the decisive battle right here.

When he heard the tortured screeching from the main gate, he knew the time had finally come.

Lindsey watched the gate's door begin to buckle, and ordered her MechWarriors to concentrate their fire on that corner. Laser and PPC fire cut through the remaining supports, and the heavy door sagged and fell forward, crushing the remains of a Canopian *Anubis* whose pilot had long since ejected.

"Forward!" she ordered, heedless of the heavy fire coming through the open doorway. If she could get even a portion of her unit back into the compound, she would be able to use it as a defensive position from which she could rally the rest of the Capellan task force back toward victory.

But things were looking grim. Warrior House Imarra was under attack by the Grey Watch and the Sixth Fides, but the enemy seemed content to keep Imarra's warriors from supporting the Fourth MAC. Following Lindsey's orders, Qiao had sent her regiment to break the Warrior House free, but from the relative quiet of her backfield Lindsey assumed the other *sang-shao* had not completely abandoned her, leaving some of her troops to keep the Kuritans from encircling the remains of her command company.

The battle between the Fourth MAC and the Kuritans had moved far beyond vicious, devolving into a series of one-on-one battles at knife-fighting range. The tight confines of the city streets kept either side from making grand, sweeping strikes in anything larger than lance-strength, and the buildup of damaged and destroyed 'Mechs in the intersections quickly turned them into either choke points or killing fields, making high-speed maneuvers and clever ambushes the plan of the day.

Lindsey watched the first of her 'Mechs advance toward the open gate. A *Lu Wei Bing*, eager to use the close confines to its fullest extent, raised its autocannon as it rounded on a Republic *Tundra Wolf 3* she imagined must belong to Maeve Stirling, the Knight of the Republic she had heard so much about.

Unfortunately, at that moment no less than five PPC bolts streaked down the street, bathing the tight confines with a brutal bluish-white light before striking the *Lu Wei Bing*. Only three of the shots actually hit, but they were enough to slam the 'Mech into the wall nearest to the destroyed door. Although not crippled, the assault BattleMech hurried into the courtyard, desperately seeking the *Tundra Wolf* that had taken the momentary distraction to seek cover.

Turning toward the source of the PPC fire, Lindsey tightened her lips as a quartet of Highlanders 'Mechs in gray marched down the street in careful cadence. The *Awesome* in the lead was the primary source of the PPC fire, but the *Warhammer* and *Marauder* flanking it each mounted a pair of PPCs. The *Archer* that followed in their wake, covering the side streets as they moved, seemed almost an afterthought.

Unfortunately, that put her troops in a very difficult position. Most of her 'Mechs had been firing at the gate from a distance, wary of counterfire from the battlements or from inside the compound once the gate was breached. That put them an intersection away from the entrance, and the Grey Watch 'Mechs would charge them a heavy price for access to the compound. The worse option, however, was if her MechWarriors made it into the compound and the Grey Watch 'Mechs were at her back. While she had a slight edge in numbers, there was no gate left for her to close, and trapping herself between the entrenched Republic 'Mechs within and the rapidly approaching Grey Watch 'Mechs without was not a choice she wanted to make.

As was so often the case, circumstance changed the situation for her. A wave of missiles arrowed out at her from her left, and she felt the impacts from a half-dozen long-range missiles strike her *Pillager,* one flashing directly past her cockpit.

She took an instinctive step back, adjusting her stance to provide a more stable firing position for returning fire, and answered with a Gauss rifle shot at the Kuritan 'Mechs now edging their way around the perimeter of the compound. The *Owens* that had fired at her was only a slight annoyance, but the *Wight* following in its wake could certainly pose a much greater problem.

The decision was easy. "Command company," she broadcast, "take the compound, maximum speed! Charlie Lance, hold the intersection until we are clear."

Her first two lances rushed toward the safety of the compound. Additional fire came downrange from the approaching Grey Watch and Kurita BattleMechs, but her hopes that they might engage each other were in vain: the nearest Kurita shots cleared harmlessly over one of the Grey Watch 'Mech's shoulders.

Due to how densely packed her 'Mechs were, any missiles that missed one seemed to strike another, and she saw a withdrawing *Raven* take a hit on its beaklike nose as it attempted to barrel its way into the compound.

Suddenly, she had no more time to watch her people, as the heavier Kuritan forces grew more visible in the distance.

Under normal circumstances, she would have had the usual healthy respect for any combatant, no matter how small, but she was extremely conscious of the damage she had already taken, and her ammo reserves were partially depleted. The battle was dragging on much longer than expected, and none of the combatants seemed eager to disengage. She needed to do something to break the stalemate, and quickly.

Qiao's voice clicked on over the comm: "*Sang-shao,* we have linked up with Imarra!"

Lindsey slumped in relief as much as her safety restraints allowed, now that she could see a way out. "Can you hold your position?"

"We can do better than that." Qiao's voice held true triumph. "The Republic is pulling back, so we can push forward to relieve you."

Lindsey instantly saw what was happening, and knew what she had to do. The Grey Watch lance was not a separate unit: it was the first of the reinforcements heading to the compound. With the fresh Highlanders pushing into the city, they were hoping to dislodge her foothold completely.

With the Kuritan forces still pressing her, it might actually work.

She glanced one last time at the compound, and then activated her microphone. "Warrior House Imarra, Laurel's Legion, push forward to link up with me. First and Second Battalion, pull back to rendezvous with them. Third Battalion, provide a bulwark on the west side of the compound."

It was a hasty plan, but it might give her the opening she so desperately needed. With her relatively fresh reserves engaging the Kuritans, she should be able to hold the enemy back long enough to retake the compound. Once she did, she could use that as the linchpin to coordinate her defense of the area, and hopefully convince the Kuritans to agree to a temporary ceasefire.

It was also a long shot, but if she could get to the ComStar data at the compound, she was fairly sure she would find evidence that Cheng's shuttle explosion had not been her fault. If she could get Ikeda to slow down, even for just a minute, it would give them all a vital moment to reorganize. Hell, if she could somehow convince Ikeda that the Republic or the Highlanders were behind the attack on his DropShip, the whole tactical situation would change.

All of that, however, required her to take back the compound, and quickly.

The front ranks of her company, the ones already in the compound, pressed forward, and her lance charged in behind them.

CHAPTER 17

"I dinna care if we haena heard from 'em. I trained two of those warriors since they were wee 'uns. If they're still standin', they're still fightin'."

—Major Seamus Casey, 9 December 3150

HPG COMPOUND
TARA, NORTHWIND
REPUBLIC OF THE SPHERE
9 DECEMBER 3150

Declan swore as the Fourth MAC's command company pressed into the compound, and kept a steady barrage of fire on the new bevy of targets, alternating shots between his *Marauder II*'s PPCs and other weapons to keep his heat to a moderately painful inferno.

Declan and Jaffray had abandoned the upper battlements, taking cover in the inner courtyard among small buildings. He'd been thrilled to hear the Sixth Fides infantry had already evacuated the structures to avoid collateral damage. For the hundredth time he wondered where Bianca was, but there was no time to worry about that now.

Maeve's lance had sold themselves dearly so far, with nearly a half-dozen Capellan 'Mechs down, and they still held a defendable position. With most of the enemy's jump-capable 'Mechs defeated, they had fewer threats from above to worry about.

Unfortunately, the remaining foes were all heavy and assault 'Mechs, and while they all bore damage, they were coming with a vengeance. Stephens was down and unresponsive, his *Peacekeeper* a shattered hulk on the ground. Maeve's *Tundra Wolf* had lost one arm and was sheltered behind the main building, daring any 'Mechs to come down the tight corridor of death she had made between the heavy walls and the buildings. The sight of two shattered Capellan 'Mechs was enough to warn the others exactly what would occur to them if they tried, but it was only a matter of time before the Capellans' momentum would force them down this avenue.

On top of everything else, Maeve's lance was nearly out of ammunition. The Knight had exhausted her missiles, now relying solely on her energy weapons. Jaffray was conserving her last few Gauss rifle rounds, but she was out of LRMs and using her SRMs sparingly. Declan was down to a pair of Gauss rifle shots, and he intended to use them on something worthwhile.

The approaching *Pillager* caught his attention, and he knew what to use his remaining rounds for. The hulking 'Mech towered over the battlefield, and had to be the command 'Mech for the unit.

Lining up his shot, Declan began his assault with his twin PPCs, taking the green-and-white 'Mech in the chest, then ducked back behind the building as the space lit up with return fire from one of the *Pillager*'s companions, an 85-ton *Lu Wei Bing*.

After waiting for the lull in fire, he popped back out and fired his second-to-last Gauss rifle round, which struck the *Pillager* in the upper arm. The slug left a massive crater in the 'Mech's armor, but he took a hit from the *Pillager*'s own Gauss rifle in response, losing what little armor remained over the left side of his 'Mech's torso.

Seeing three enemy 'Mechs approaching Maeve, Declan darted back into the intersection and fired all but his last Gauss rifle shot at the *Huron Warrior* leading the charge. While its armament wasn't suited to close-range fighting, the heavy weapons it mounted could easily take down the damaged *Tundra Wolf* if the pilot got a clear shot. Both of his PPCs hit the *Huron Warrior*'s right arm, turning it into a blackened husk, and he grinned tightly as the Gauss rifle's capacitor banks blew the arm clean off the 'Mech's torso. Overbalanced by the loss of its arm and the sudden neurofeedback from the explosion, the *Huron Warrior* fell down the side alley, while the other two Capellan 'Mechs marched onward.

Declan's cockpit became an inferno, the waste heat locking up his controls and slowing his reactions. It was just what the incoming *Pillager* had been waiting for, and its other Gauss rifle blasted his 'Mech's left arm away in a spray of broken armor and torn myomer bundles. Fighting the sway from the loss of so much tonnage, Declan forced all his concentration on keeping his balance, especially as a second salvo of heavy fire took him in the leg, breaching the armor.

That also meant his firepower would be more than halved when he fired his last Gauss rifle round.

As he finally ducked back behind the building, he found the damage had been worth it. Jaffray had engaged one of the other 'Mechs, and Maeve had popped out to savage her ambushers. Left alone where three once stood, the final Capellan 'Mech, a *Wraith*, decided that pulling back was the better part of survival, and jumped toward the wall.

Unfortunately, that still left the Capellan commander with a lance of 'Mechs against Maeve's three critically damaged ones.

Which, as always, was when the Highlanders came to call.

"Knight Lance, get out of here!" Colonel Griffin's voice rang clear as he shouldered his way into the compound. Several Capellan 'Mechs turned and fired at his *Awesome*, but the 80-ton assault 'Mech's thick armor shrugged off the damage with little effort.

Maeve's voice sounded breathy, a clear sign the heat in her cockpit was at dangerous levels. "We can hold—"

"No, you can't." The colonel's voice was clear, and Declan watched a pair of Maxim hover transports shot into the compound, moving so fast that one of the clipped the side of a building as they pulled up next to the main structure. "By order of the countess, we are abandoning the HPG. You need to get out of here, *now*."

Before Declan could reply, Griffin fired all of his PPCs at the *Pillager*, striking it in the chest and arm, then he fired again.

Firing like a man who did not care whether he would survive.

The *Pillager*'s armor was starting to give way, and the Capellan pilot returned fire with the 'Mech's full complement. Both Gauss rifle slugs gouged deep into the *Awesome*'s chest, the lasers doing little more than carving some armor from either arm.

In that moment, Declan saw Maeve's ejection seat rocket skyward. While he had been concentrating on the *Pillager*, the *Wraith* had jumped back toward Maeve, and the two 'Mechs had traded a final alpha strike that destroyed them both. Her *Tundra Wolf*'s fusion engine had been cored, and the Capellan 'Mech had a smoking crater where its head had been.

He watched Maeve's ejection seat sail out of the compound, and immediately sent out an urgent message to confirm someone was tracking her as he saw her parachute deploy. One of the APCs outside of the walls reported they were on search and rescue, and he concentrated back on the battle at hand.

The remaining three Capellan 'Mechs were all engaged. The *Pillager* was locked in combat with the *Awesome*, Jaffray traded shots with the *Lu Wei Bing*, and Declan found a *Shen Yi* stalking him, the heavy 'Mech showing up as a blurry smudge on his sensors, thanks to its stealth armor.

Amid the battle, Declan saw a third Maxim transport speed into the compound, taking the occupants of the first two Maxims and what few Sixth Fides infantry remained, then spun around and headed back out, aiming for the open gate, and made to escape.

As the *Shen Yi* moved to fire at it, Seamus' *Marauder* rushed into the compound, firing its PPCs in quick succession. Only one shot hit the smaller 'Mech, inflicting no noticeable damage, but it threw off the *Shen Yi*'s aim long enough for the hover transport to make its escape.

Declan stifled a quick burst of panic as he sidestepped and twisted his torso to bring the *Shen Yi* into his crosshairs. As talented a MechWarrior as his grandfather was, that old *Marauder* was at a severe disadvantage in a close-range battle with the more advanced BattleMech, and it was vital that Declan take down Seamus' opponent before it could react to this new threat.

"Dec!" Seamus shouted over the comm. "Get the hell outta there!"

But Declan pressed forward and fired his remaining weapons at the *Shen Yi*, including his final Gauss rifle round. The PPC struck his target's right leg, but a combination of the Capellan 'Mech's stealth armor and the mounting heat in his cockpit guaranteed that the other weapons missed.

The *Shen Yi* did not hesitate. With Declan's larger 'Mech in its sights, it lashed out with its ER large laser, which carved armor from his less damaged leg. Declan would have breathed a sigh of relief, but he was suddenly engulfed in a tumult of forty medium-range missiles. The swarm blasted armor from his 'Mech's chest and head, and ripped the right arm off his 'Mech.

That was it. With the loss of his remaining arm, Declan had no remaining weapons, and few remaining options. Throttling up his 'Mech to a run, he aimed directly at the *Shen Yi* in one final act of defiance.

He charged the *Shen Yi* at full speed, closing the distance between them. Beside him, he saw a flash of weapons fire as the *Awesome* and *Pillager* dueled each other like two massive titans locked in mortal combat. One of the *Awesome*'s PPCs savaged the *Pillager*'s left arm, ripping off part of its Gauss rifle barrel.

At a dead run, Seamus' *Marauder* struck the *Shen Yi* as it turned. He charged forward to knock it out of the way, sending it into the larger two 'Mechs. The *Shen Yi* recovered long enough to unload all of its weapons into the bird-like *Marauder*'s chest at point-blank range.

Declan turned to assist his grandfather, but the effort of keeping his heavily damaged 'Mech upright at a full run amid the sudden shift in the battlefield caused him to skid on the ferrocrete. He crashed to the ground, rattling every bone in his body as his 'Mech skidded toward the compound's gate.

From his sideways orientation, he saw the falling *Shen Yi* slam into the *Pillager*'s other Gauss rifle, and the collision sparked a capacitor explosion that activated the *Pillager*'s auto-eject. The four 'Mechs fell into a desperate tangle as Declan desperately tried to wrestle control of his skidding 'Mech and search Seamus' *Marauder* for some sign of life.

He'd managed to reach a partially crouched position when a blinding explosion from the HPG blotted out his vision. His entire world shifted around him.

Then everything went black.

It took all of Ikeda's self-control to keep from roaring in sheer rage as he witnessed the fireball leap up from the HPG compound. The blast engulfed the dish and the outlying buildings in a series of chained explosions, sending columns of reddish-orange fire skyward. The heavy walls around the compound had shielded most of the forces outside, but they also contained the shockwave, which deformed the HPG's framework and shattered the glass and stone buildings that had survived the initial detonation. Moments later, the HPG dish slumped forward as if in exhaustion, its motion controls heavily damaged.

Ikeda instantly knew this was more Capellan treachery. If they could not have the HPG, they had decided no one else would as well. While he thought that was fair for their enemies, the Capellans were supposed to be his allies!

Taking advantage of the momentary lull in the conflict after the destruction of the HPG compound, Ikeda surveyed the wreckage. Most of the buildings had been completely destroyed, and while the walls protecting the compound still stood, massive chunks had torn free, leaving gaps where he could still see fires burning inside the compound.

Turning away from the devastation, he made a quick call to his command center to verify the data in front of him and request a status update on his other units. The reports he received confirmed his own analysis. His troops had taken significant damage, but were still combat capable, and the signal that HPGs emitted to confirm their operation was gone.

Northwind had been cut off from communications with the larger universe.

On top of that, the Highlanders had recently reached the battlefield, intent on holding the city, and they were relatively fresh. He was confident the Fourth Dieron Regulars, still relatively unbloodied themselves, could defeat them, but courting a new enemy was never wise, especially for no worthwhile goal.

His first instinct was to finish off the traitorous Capellan forces, but prudence told him it would be far more important to immediately bring word of this treachery back to the Coordinator.

"All Kurita forces, withdraw to the DropShips," Ikeda ordered. He would later consult with his aides and look at the strategic situation from a carefully calculated distance, and then he would decide on a course of action. But all signs pointed to a return home.

As his troops began withdrawing, Ikeda spared one last look at the plumes of smoke drifting up from the ruined HPG before turning his *Tai-sho* to follow them.

There is nothing left to fight for here. The best path to serve the Dragon is to leave this beleaguered planet behind.

CHAPTER 18

"Following the extraordinary events of the last twenty-four hours, a tentative calm has fallen over the city of Tara. After the explosion that occurred at the HPG compound, the Kuritan and Capellan forces have both withdrawn from the city center, and Republic forces have spread out to reclaim the city. Time will only tell what will happen next..."

—Tegan Shea, *Northwind Today*, 10 December 3150

OVERLORD-CLASS DROPSHIP *TALON ZAHN*
KOHLER SPACEPORT
TARA, NORTHWIND
REPUBLIC OF THE SPHERE
10 DECEMBER 3150

Lindsey Baxter opened her eyes slowly, turning her head away from the harsh, blinding light, and then shut them tightly until she could acclimate to the sudden brightness. The lights in the room dimmed, allowing her to finally crack her eyes open again, and she made out the nearby form of a tall man in a white coat.

"Give your eyes a little time to adjust," the unfamiliar voice said. "You have been out for several hours. You have suffered neurofeedback shock, so you may feel some continued disorientation."

"Where am I?" she asked, her lips and tongue feeling as if they were made of sandpaper.

"You are on the *Talon Zahn*, *Sang-shao*. *Sang-shao* Qiao ordered us to bring you aboard when the S&R teams recovered you from the battlefield. My name is Armand Jackson, and I am the physician in charge of your care at the moment."

Lindsey nodded, vaguely remembering the armored infantry cutting her out of the straps on her ejected command couch while the rest of her lance provided covering fire. "My company...?"

"They pulled back to the spaceport with the rest of our forces."

This time her discomfort was completely internal. If they had withdrawn to the DropShips, it meant Tara was no longer in Capellan hands. Suddenly, she remembered the blinding flash coming from the HPG compound, and how the ground had seemed to heave up beneath her. "The HPG?"

"The whole compound has been destroyed," the young doctor replied.

Lindsey screwed her eyes shut against the wave of anguish. Despite all of their efforts, they had failed to hold the HPG, and now that failure had cost the Confederation a vital strategic resource. "Can you give me a status report?"

"I believe *Sang-shao* Qiao is already on her way," Jackson replied.

Lindsey nodded slowly, taking a moment to gather her thoughts before her friend arrived. If they were at the DropShips, Qiao had likely gone with their primary contingency plan, circling the wagons to maximize their options should things take a dangerous turn. While she had never truly believed they would need to enact this contingency, Lindsey knew better than to go into battle without an exit strategy.

Her thoughts were interrupted as Julie entered the room, *Shiao-zhang* Garzon in her wake. Lindsey was gratified to see the glimpse of true concern on the other woman's face before a grateful smile wiped it away.

"I'm glad to see you back to the world of the living, *Sang-shao*," Qiao said.

Lindsey gave a wan smile in reply. "It was quite the journey, I assure you. How are we looking?"

"We have moved to Contingency Plan Alpha." Qiao's expression turned grave. "When you ejected, I had my forces make a push at the Republic and the Highlanders, giving us enough breathing room to withdraw in good order. All of our units now surround the spaceport, and the DropShips will give us additional firepower to push back the Republic forces, should they attempt to dislodge us."

Lindsey nodded, but understood what Qiao hadn't said. Now that the Republic controlled most of the city again, they could afford to wait without risking further damage by attempting to seize the spaceport. Lindsey's troops could only survive on their stockpile of supplies for so long. "What about the Combine forces?"

There was a pregnant pause before Qiao spoke. "They are pulling out of the combat theater. The majority of them have already boarded their DropShips and burned for orbit."

Lindsey nodded slowly. For the Combine, the destruction of the HPG must have finally tipped the scales, making them decide that further action would gain them nothing. With the loss of the HPG, the prize they both coveted had been removed from play, removing any further justification for staying. By pulling out of the area, the Combine had left the situation as it had begun: between the Republic forces and her own.

"Did they say anything before they departed?"

Once again, there was the careful look, and Qiao's gaze flickered to the House Imarra commander. "They sent a message before they left the city."

Lindsey gestured to Jackson, who came over to raise the bed to a seated position. "Do you have a copy?"

Qiao nodded, and slipped a small data disk into the large monitor on the opposite wall. She had come prepared, despite the fact that she was hesitant to let her friend see the message.

Hisao Ikeda's imposing visage appeared on the screen. "*Sang-shao* Baxter." His voice was carefully measured as always, but a hint of the rage she had heard from their last conversation still colored his tone. "I will admit, when I heard that your units were retreating back to the safety of your DropShips, I was tempted to continue forward, to remind you of what you had lost by attacking your allies. However, I decided it would be a far more fitting punishment to allow you to stay and wither upon the vine, crushed by your own hubris when the Republic forces finally drive you from this planet.

"You have finally received your wish: we involved ourselves in your battle with the Republic. Yet you made a grave miscalculation, *Sang-shao*, and a terrible enemy. I leave your nation to its perfidy, and you should pray that the Hikage are always fighting more worthy prey, so that we may never cross paths again." The *sho-sho* focused on the screen one last time, burning a deadly glare into the holovid camera, and then he cut the connection with a wave of his hand.

"Good riddance," Qiao replied in the long silence that followed. "If they had only—"

"There is no time for regrets," Lindsey interrupted. "What is our current status?"

"As of this moment, my regiment is guarding the perimeter of the spaceport, with Warrior House Imarra as our primary response force, should it be needed. The majority of the Fourth is currently rearming, and I had the remaining Canopians board the DropShips, as they have been shattered for the purposes of command and control. Several of their 'Mechs may be viable to continue fighting, but I didn't want to risk combat-loss grouping until we were sure that they could be effective." Qiao's expression darkened. "Colonel Centrella-Tompkins is MIA."

A pang of regret for the Canopian commander stabbed Lindsey, and she nodded silently.

"We can push back into the city at any time," Qiao continued, "and I would recommend we do so sooner rather than later. The Republic forces are tightening their grip on the city, but they have made no move against us yet."

"I doubt that will happen," Lindsey replied, as she looked between Qiao and Garzon. "They know we won't be staying long."

"What?" Garzon did not bother to hide his surprise. "You are considering abandoning the planet?"

"I feel there is no other viable alternative. We might be able to retake the city or even take advantage of our own mobility to attack the Castle before their own forces can get into place to supplement them, but the greater question to ask ourselves is exactly what would we accomplish? Without the HPG, the city holds little intrinsic value, and due to some of our units' actions within the city..." She was careful not to look at Garzon, who had the good sense to look abashed. "...its populace is up in arms against us. I could easily see us being picked apart by partisans as we try to tighten our grip here, which would only serve to deplete our strength further."

"We could tie down the Republic forces..." Qiao began softly, but Lindsey shook her head.

"Perhaps we could, but I think the majority of the Republic forces are going to be returning to their own JumpShips as soon as Ikeda's troops leave the system. Stone's Defenders and the Sixth Fides accomplished what they came here to do, but Terra is going to need them sooner rather than later. Tying them down here is a mixed bag: sure, we could do it, but that would also prevent us from taking part in any offensive actions on a different front. The Celestial Wisdom made it very clear he had no additional forces to spare, and we have instructions to return home should the mission become unviable. With the damage we have already taken, and the lack of additional benefit to staying, there is little reason to remain."

"I concur," came a voice from the doorway.

All three officers straightened in surprise as *Gao-shiao-zhang* Hui strolled into the room gingerly, moving with a slow, careful gait meant to hide the extent of his wounds. He gave them all a fair approximation of his usual smile, shifting his gaze between them. "While it galls me that we have not achieved all of our objectives, we need to acknowledge how much we have done, and focus on our own victories."

"Our own victories, Master?" Garzon asked, clearly embarrassed to not have known his commander was up and about.

"Yes, *Lien-zhang*," the *gao-shiao-zhang* said with a smile, using Garzon's original rank. "We have denied the Republic three of their best units for a time, and we managed to deny them the command-and-control capabilities to strike into our own nation. We have single-handedly ended the Republic threat to our borders. While I doubt we will be moving forward into the Republic as the Chancellor had hoped, we have accomplished something great here, and I will ensure that the Celestial Wisdom is well aware of how it was done.

"We also need to be very clear about the duplicity of our supposed allies," Hui continued. "By withholding their aid, we were forced to take different steps than I would have hoped, which kept us from making further gains. That information alone will be invaluable to the Chancellor, and I have no doubt we will be seeing some fairly major repercussions from *Sho-sho* Ikeda's actions here.

"All in all, it was not the complete victory we were hoping for. Still, we managed to protect the Confederation, and our efforts will allow us to prepare for the threat to our great nation, no matter who might conquer Terra.

"However, there are still a few loose ends that we must tie up." Hui's smile was fleeting. "Where is the Maskirovka liaison?"

Garzon looked sheepish, but something in his gaze filled Lindsey with suspicion. "Unfortunately, it appears he slipped out in the middle of the battle. As best we can tell, he was never on the shuttle that exploded on the Kuritan flagship, but we have found no trace of him on-planet. I have informed all commands to keep a lookout for him, but I fear he has gone to ground, and we do not have the resources to spare to hunt for him."

"Just so," the *gao-shiao-zhang* replied, and now Lindsey was fairly sure she saw a small flicker of something in his eyes. With the destruction of the HPG, any messages for the Chancellor would be sent via a JumpShip courier instead, and she knew the *gao-shiao-zhang* would get to tell his side of the story long before any report that would contradict him could come down the pipeline. For now, though, her goal was merely to continue forward, and leave that for another day."

"That settles that, at least, but there is another issue." Hui focused on Garzon. "You disobeyed my implicit directives to leave the Highlanders' dependents alone."

"I used the methods I thought were best," Garzon replied carefully, and he faced his Grand Master unflinchingly. "Unfortunately, I chose my allies poorly: I allowed Agent Cheng to influence my plans, and in so doing led to our defeat. I recognize my folly, and I stand ready to accept my punishment."

"Your statements are understood, but *I* am not the one you have truly wronged," the *gao-shiao-zhang* replied.

Garzon wrinkled his brow for a moment, and then turned to Lindsey. "*Sang-shao* Baxter, I have erred and caused your unit damage. I stand ready to atone for my failures."

She caught Hui's eye, and gave him a quick smile of agreement when she realized what he was thinking, although Garzon would not have seen it. "I am glad you recognize the repercussions of your actions, *Lien-zhang*," she said. "I have indeed lost good soldiers in this campaign due to your decisions, but I understand you came by them honestly."

"Still..." Hui interjected, "atonement must be made. *Lien-zhang*, you are now seconded to the Fourth McCarron's Armored Cavalry until you have worked off your debt of honor, or until Warrior House Imarra decides to take you back."

The now-former House Warrior bowed deeply, a mixture of relief and loss at the punishment rendered. Clearly he had expected to pay for his transgressions with his life, but the Grand Master had offered him a different way out.

"*Gao-shiao-zhang*, do you have a recommendation for our next steps?" Qiao asked.

Hui smiled tightly, but shook his head. "I am still technically under a physician's care, as is *Sang-shao* Baxter. You have done an excellent job protecting us for the time being, so you are more than capable of handling the preparations for our departure."

Qiao puffed up, the gratitude in her eyes more expansive than anything Lindsey could have said, and straightened to attention. With a proud nod, she departed, and a flicker of a glance ensured that Garzon departed as well, leaving the *gao-shiao-zhang* alone with Lindsey.

Hui gingerly shuffled to the chair beside the bed, and sat down with a grateful sigh. Lindsey straightened in her bed, taking the Grand Master's admission of his injury as a gesture of trust.

Which made it even more startling when Hui's head snapped up in surprise as she swore, just loudly enough not to be heard beyond the confines of the room.

"*Sang-shao—*"

Lindsey shook her head, cutting him off before he could continue. "Please, *Gao-shiao-zhang*, please don't. We both know the truth: no matter how we choose to spin it to the others, this was a defeat."

My defeat.

"Do not underestimate the power of spin, *Sang-shao*," Hui said. "Our reports will be read at the highest level of the state, and everyone will see the truth of it. Yes, we did lose the HPG, but you accomplished all of your initial goals, for a short time at least—a fact I will be mentioning prominently in my report. While we were unable to hold the HPG compound, we also denied it to the Republic and the Combine, and that was a worthy objective in and of itself."

"Somehow, I doubt the Chancellor will see it that way," Lindsey retorted. "He specifically tasked me with this mission, and I have failed him. I will be lucky if he only cashiers me." *Who am I kidding? For a failure of this magnitude, the best-case scenario is that he only executes me, and allows a new commander to attempt to redeem the honor of the regiment.*

"Perhaps. But do not forget that the Celestial Wisdom also sees the value in all of his subjects. While you may suffer for your defeat now, I do not doubt he will find a path toward your own redemption."

For the briefest of moments, Lindsey allowed herself to take solace in the elder warrior's words, but then she felt it all crash back down on her. *Pretty words, as always, but this was my chance at redemption...and I failed.*

Hui continued despite the expression on her face. "You also showed that our 'allies' from the Draconis Combine were contemplating treachery from the start. With the Federated Suns on the brink of destruction, we may be facing our erstwhile allies sooner than later. That is vital intelligence, and the Chancellor will not forget that you were the one who provided it to him."

The mention of intelligence was enough to make Lindsey straighten, a harsh expression crossing her features, and Hui nodded. "Speaking of intelligence, it also must be mentioned that our losses were not due to our own actions alone. Clearly Mr. Cheng had his own agenda, and it forced our hand. If he was, as I suspect, behind the mysterious explosion that damaged the Kuritan flagship, his actions were the catalyst to destroying our relations with the Combine."

For a brief moment, Lindsey allowed herself the brief pleasure of considering what she would do to Maxwell Cheng if she ever got her hands on him, but then a wave of crushing despair swept over her, wrenching her back to the present. She shook her head in an attempt to clear it, focusing once more on the Grand Master. *How can I make him understand?*

"I appreciate your words, *Gao-shiao-zhang*, but I fear that neither the Chancellor nor my commanding officer will be nearly so forgiving in their analysis of the mission."

Hui shook his head. "You forget, *Sang-shao*: I know Cyrus McCarron fairly well, and he will be hearing directly from me. There is no dishonor to be found in either your deeds or your results. I have no doubt the Chancellor will not be fully pleased with the results, but he can take solace in the fact that the best units did their utmost for him, and that will be remembered."

No. Baxter thought to herself, the Grand Master's patronizing words cutting her right to the core. *The* gao-shiao-zhang *may see this is as just another setback, and for him it might just be, but this was a failure.* My *failure.* I *lost the HPG.* I *allowed the Republic to drive me from the city.* I *allowed the Unity Pact to break down...* All of these failures could be laid only at her doorstep. She shook her head, her course of action clear. *When I see the Chancellor again, I will supplicate myself abjectly before him, in the hopes that he would not place the blame for my failures on my regiment as a whole.*

Despite all of these thoughts, she gave Hui a small nod of gratitude. "Thank you, *Gao-shiao-zhang.*"

For a moment, it seemed the Grand Master had more to say, but instead he simply nodded and stepped out of the room without saying another word, leaving Lindsey alone with her troubled thoughts.

CHAPTER 19

"Victory, yes. But at what cost?"

—Countess Tara Campbell, 10 December 3150

TARA GENERAL HOSPITAL
TARA, NORTHWIND
REPUBLIC OF THE SPHERE
10 DECEMBER 3150

In the corner of the hospital room, Declan sat quietly in the comfortable armchair, a luxury that must have been brought from another floor, probably the maternity ward. Across the room, Bianca Haller lay quietly; her breathing and the slow beeping of the machines keeping her alive were the only sounds in the room.

A search and rescue unit had pulled him from the cockpit of his *Marauder II*, which had been covered in debris from the explosion. While he felt fine, the medics had insisted on taking him back to the prefab building they were using as a triage center. He had found Bianca there, still unconscious, having been rescued from the control room when the Sixth Fides infantry had retaken the space. She had been one of the lucky few of her team to survive, as the Fourth MAC's infantry had made a vicious attempt to retake the control room.

Following the explosion that had torn through the compound, the Kuritan forces had pulled back in good order, careful to take a route that kept them clear of the approaching Highlanders, who had little interest in them. With the Kuritans en route to their DropShips, the Highlanders and Republic forces quickly retook the majority of the city, while the Capellans continued to pull back and regroup at the spaceport. The countess had ordered the Highlanders and remaining Twelfth Hastati to pace the Capellans at a safe distance in case they decided to make a push to retake the city, but the Capellans had apparently decided to consolidate their forces instead of getting bogged down in another battle so soon.

From the data the Republic forces were getting, it seemed a wise choice. The Kuritans had hammered the Fourth MAC during the fight at the HPG compound, although they still remained functionally intact. The First Canopian Lancers had suffered many casualties, including the loss of their commander. Warrior House Imarra and Laurel's Legion had both taken damage, but they seemed content to hold the perimeter of the spaceport for now, allowing the other Capellan units to repair and rearm. The Capellans had set up a powerful defensive position at the spaceport, but the ranks of the planet's defenders, now able to consolidate to face the invaders head on, was impressive.

Things were looking moderately better for the Republic forces. Stone's Defenders were untouched, having held station during the conflict, although the Highlanders, both the Grey Watch and Tara Campbell's battalion, had taken a beating within the city. The Twelfth Hastati had never fully recovered from the battle at the Castle, and they would need some major reorganization before they could be fielded intact again.

All of this had led to the current tense stalemate. Both forces were now relatively equal in strength, but a conflict would take everything they had if the Capellans attempted a breakout and forced the Highlanders to keep them out of the city again. Luckily, neither side wanted to push the issue yet, which let both sides rest and rearm while the Highlanders brought in their limited artillery assets to cover the Capellans' position within the spaceport. For several hours, it seemed the conflict would start back up in earnest.

Then the Capellans departed, without so much as a message as to their intentions. While the local media was playing it up as the enemy running off with their tails between their legs, Declan knew the enemy could still have made a fight of it. By departing after the loss of the HPG, it sent the message that the Confederation no longer saw the Republic as a threat.

Deep down, although he would never admit it, Declan wondered if they might be right.

Because his grandfather was dead.

And it was all because of him.

He could not get over was the sheer capriciousness of it all. From what he had been told, the remains of one of the HPG compound's outer buildings had shielded him from the majority of the blast, his *Marauder II*'s armor holding up just long enough to protect him through the explosions. Colonel Griffin also survived, the legendary armor of his *Awesome* living up to its name, and intelligence reports claimed at least one Capellan warrior had survived the blast.

They had survived, but Seamus...

Declan stood abruptly, careful not to disturb Bianca, and moved away from the bed, tears stinging the edges of his eyes. All he could think about was the gruff way he had treated Seamus the last few days, all of the opportunities for the two of them to talk that would now never occur, how he had been so wrapped up in his own nonsense that he hadn't recognized how precious their time together was.

Yet that had not stopped his grandfather from storming into an enemy-held position against vastly superior forces without a thought for his own safety. Taking the fight directly to enemy BattleMechs several generations more advanced, and piloting an iconic BattleMech that had seen too many battles, too much damage...

Too much death.

Declan had visited Colonel Griffin in the hospital, where he was recovering from his own wounds. The colonel had asked for him personally, and he had gone, although it was the last thing he truly wanted to do.

Declan knew it wasn't right to resent the colonel, just because he had lived while Seamus had not. Even more importantly, Seamus Casey had thought the world of Michael Griffin, and Declan refused to dishonor the memory of his grandfather by taking it out on the colonel.

So he went, expecting to hear how his grandfather was a great man, how he could never be replaced. All things he already knew, and now cursed to never forget.

To his surprise, upon arriving at the hospital room, he had been met by Countess Campbell, Colonel Griffin, and Lieutenant Colonel Jaffray. While they had wanted to offer their condolences, the purpose of their invitation was to offer him a new assignment.

The Highlanders were leaving Northwind and returning to Terra to defend the heart of the Republic. While Declan had always expected that, he had given no thought to who would go with them. The Twelfth Hastati Sentinels could not go: though damaged, the regiment was still the official Republic garrison force for Northwind, responsible for its defense. Campbell's Highlanders had also taken a bit of a beating in their time on the planet. As such, a battalion of the Grey Watch would accompany the countess back to Terra, to round out her numbers and show honor to both their Republic allies and their foes.

Unfortunately, that left the Grey Watch with a serious logistical problem. The regiment had suffered fairly serious losses of its own, and there was not only the problem of rebuilding to full strength, but readjusting their defensive procedures, now that many of their surprises had been sprung. While it was Declan's fondest hope that there would not be another battle of Northwind in his lifetime, the planet had seen too much conflict over the decades for him to be sure of anything.

Therefore, the Grey Watch wanted him to assist in the rebuilding. Colonel Griffin had to go to Terra, as a symbolic gesture if nothing else, and Jaffray chose to accompany him, to provide another command presence, especially since Griffin's injuries might not let him lead from the field in the near future. With both Lieutenant Colonel Halloran and Declan's grandfather dead, the Grey Watch would have serious holes in its senior leadership while Griffin and Jaffray were absent.

Griffin had promoted the next senior member of the Grey Watch, Major Eric McCormack, to oversee the rebuilding, but he would need help. The colonel explained that having another Northwind Highlander in the ranks would not hurt...and hearing that a "Major Casey" was on duty would be exactly the sort of stability the wounded regiment needed.

Declan had accepted the assignment without question.

A quiet voice came from the doorway, interrupting his thoughts.

"How is she doing?" Standing just outside the door, Maeve was wearing the gray uniform Declan recalled from their first meeting, not the MechWarrior togs he had gotten used to seeing her in.

Not wanting to disturb Bianca, Declan stepped into the hallway. He took a brief moment to hide his distress about Seamus before replying. "Bianca is doing well, still a bit out of it. She took a glancing blow during the battle when the Sixth Fides retook the control room."

Maeve nodded. "She's pretty tough, that one."

"That she is."

"Oh, I thought you should know... The murderer you were looking for, the one suspected of killing the NMA's commandant? They found out who did it."

"Halloran?" Declan asked idly, smiling slightly as the Knight whipped her head around in surprise.

"You knew?"

"I suspected. He seemed so eager to get into battle back when the NMA was threatened, so focused on redeeming himself, but then his mood shifted when the siege was finally lifted. I knew there had to be something more to it."

Maeve nodded slowly. "They found a note in his room: He had quarreled with the commandant..."

"The former Grey Watch leader," Declan said, "about assisting in the Steel Wolf attack."

"You seem to know quite a bit about this," she stated, a hint of suspicion creeping into her voice. "Should I even bother to go on?"

"It makes sense if you think about it," Declan explained. "It's the one question we never had the time to truly explore due to the Capellan threat: Why was the Grey Watch not deployed when the Steel Wolves attacked Northwind the first time?"

Maeve nodded. "I am guessing you have come up with the solution?"

"I think so. At the time, no one imagined the Steel Wolves would jump for Terra. It was a blind spot on the Exarch's part, but it was one we shared. Everyone, including the Grey Watch, thought the Steel Wolves were going to press forward to try to conquer Northwind."

"Which meant the Grey Watch had to be prepared to counterstrike when the Steel Wolves weren't concentrated," Maeve replied.

"That's what the argument was about, I am guessing," Declan replied. "Lieutenant Colonel Halloran was always a firebrand, so he would've wanted to strike immediately, but the commandant was far more cautious. It made them a good command team, but I could certainly see the commandant saying that committing their forces too soon would be premature. Since the Grey Watch worked off a decentralized cell system, it would have taken time for any orders to get to all the various lances. When they didn't receive the orders to move..."

"They didn't move," she finished. "Until the commandant was killed."

"Exactly. Jaffray was too junior to her position to have known about the disagreement, as was my grandfather. That also raised another point: both of them retired at the same time, so why were both higher in the new command structure than Halloran...unless there was a question as to his loyalties?"

Declan smiled slightly. "It also says a great deal that Griffin was put in charge of the regiment, not Halloran, Jaffray, or my grandfather..."

"They couldn't be trusted to put the Republic's goals over the Highlanders," Maeve said with a nod. "Griffin could."

"They couldn't be trusted to put the *Exarch*'s goals over Northwind's," Declan corrected. "So they needed someone a little more compatible for their goals: the Countess was needed elsewhere, so they co-opted Griffin upon his return."

"Plans within plans," Maeve said.

"Always," Declan agreed. "So what's the plan now?"

"With the Capellans burning for the jump point, most of the troops Countess Campbell brought with her will jump out to Terra when they receive word."

"They're not worried about the Kuritans or Capellans doubling back?"

"The countess considered it unlikely. With the salvage you received and the equipment we are leaving, you should be more than able to deal with any renewed threat from either of them, and for now we are leaving one JumpShip with the majority of our aerospace contingent. If anyone returns, you will have an early warning and one hell of a first punch to deliver."

"Won't those forces be needed on Terra?"

"Oh, they will be with us soon enough," Maeve replied with a smile. "We will only keep them here long enough to ensure that neither the Capellans or Kuritans get cute and try to turn back on us. Then, unfortunately, we are going to be on to the next battle."

"Terra."

She nodded. "It's the big showdown, it seems. Everything the Republic has fought for, coming down to a single planet. That's how it's always seemed to be, hasn't it?"

The two stood quietly for a moment, staring through the door at the injured young woman lying motionless on the bed.

"You could always stay here, you know," Declan said after a long moment. "You're a Highlander. You will always have a place here."

She smiled at him, a curiously shy gesture, but shook her head. "I swore an oath to the Republic to see this through. I don't know what we might find on Terra, but I am fairly sure it will change everything. If it does...I need to be ready for it."

"And if whatever it is proves to be a threat to Northwind?"

She raised her chin slightly, her eyes sparkling with a careful fire. "Then I will be back, of course."

"Of course," he said, sharing her smile.

Maeve glanced back into the room. "Give her my best, won't you? We couldn't have done this without her."

"I will," Declan replied.

Maeve turned slightly as if to go, but then stopped. "I suppose I should give this back to you, then." She carefully removed the Casey family blade from the sheath at her waist and handed it to him, hilt first.

Declan took the dagger with an almost reverent touch. He nodded as he felt its familiar heft, and their eyes locked for a moment.

"Thank you," he replied formally. "It will go quite nicely with the knife you left in my back."

Maeve was silent in the face of his accusation, and her gaze dipped to the blade in Declan's hand. "Are you planning to use that right now?"

"Before all of this went down...I might have." Declan looked down at the dagger, though his grip on the weapon did not loosen for even an instant. "But what's done is done, so it wouldn't serve any real purpose."

He looked back up at her, his eyes smoldering. "I figured it out on the way here, although it took me a lot longer than it should have. I was so focused on the attacks that I couldn't see the rest of the board."

"And you do now?" she asked.

"I think I do."

"Then explain it to me."

"The Capellans...they were never the real threat, were they?" His eyes narrowed as they stayed locked on her own, searching for any hint of deception. "At least, not all of it."

"Correct," she replied.

"The Unity Pact."

Maeve nodded. "The Capellans, regardless of the forces they have on hand, might be able to take Terra, but they never would have been able to hold it. The Draconis Combine assisting them, however, would have been a completely different ballgame. Even if the Combine military could not provide forces directly for a campaign to take Terra, they could easily cause problems for the supply chains of any Clan attempting to take Terra, forcing them to move resources to their backfield to protect their assets. It might not change too much in the long run, especially if one of the Clans does become the ilClan, but it would have dovetailed with the Combine mindset of pulling a victory from someone else." She looked at him squarely. "We have ensured that that will never happen. After an attack on the Combine's honor like the Capellan forces pulled here, the Unity Pact will likely be hanging by a thread, especially once the Coordinator learns what happened here."

"And the Highlanders provided you the opportunity to neuter one of the main threats to the Republic."

"I would say the Capellan Chancellor handed us the opportunity, but it would have been the height of foolishness to ignore it once it arrived."

"So all of this...it was just to negate a single threat to Terra?"

"Not at all," she replied, and her gaze hardened. "For all your attempts to look at the bigger picture, you are not taking the long view. Do you remember what we discussed that first night, in the woods?"

"The Highlanders, and how they had been betrayed. Much like you—"

"*No.*" Her voice was firm enough to stop him. "We talked how things kept failing for the Highlanders' allies because they did not treat honestly with us. They didn't maintain their covenants, didn't abide by their words. That was their flaw...one I was determined not to repeat." She looked at him, with something raw in her expression. "No matter what happens from here, the Exarch kept his covenant with us. He may have done it out of a sense of enlightened self-interest, but that doesn't change the fact that it happened."

Declan straightened, and something in his gaze caused her to give him a slow smile.

"Now you see it," she said.

"This was never about any of that...at least, not completely."

"No. This was just one of many, many contingency plans."

"You think Terra might fall."

"If Terra falls, it will be because too many people have too much invested in its failure. It should not be a repudiation of all we achieved since the Jihad, all of the good we have done. They say the history of the Inner Sphere...of humanity...is broken up by its wars. That may be true, but we also need to remember the times of peace in between, of the generations who were able to be born, live, and die under the knowledge that their entire lives need not be defined by warfare. If the Republic falls..."

She hesitated, and then stared directly at him, as if the effort would hide the watery nature of her eyes. "If the Republic falls, I want it to be with the knowledge that we accomplished something here, something that will be remembered and appreciated for all time. That the Republic Era was not just a footnote in the history of humanity, but a time when we did something grand...even if it was just for a short while."

Declan stepped back, and she took a deep breath as he lowered the dagger to his side.

"How much of this did you plan?" he asked, his eyes boring into her.

"If you're asking whether I planned this entire thing out, specifically for this sort of outcome, I think you have a massively inflated opinion of my abilities," Maeve replied, her expression amused.

"I think you know a lot more about what's going on here than you're admitting," he said simply, and he saw anger flash in her eyes for a moment. Once again, he felt the way he had on their first conversation in the Caithness Woods, slightly thrown off guard by her obfuscations and secrets, but facing it head on, as a true Highlander would. "Was this all part of your plan to see the HPG destroyed? To reveal the existence of the Grey Watch? Are you even really returning to Terra?"

The questions struck her like a physical blow, and her anger suddenly returned in full force. "I am going back to protect Terra as is required of my oath, Declan. I don't know if I'll survive, or if I do, whether I'll ever be able to return to Northwind again. However, I had the chance to fight for my homeworld, alongside some of the finest warriors I have ever known. I have done my duty, and I am content."

"However..." She caught his attention, and their eyes locked for a long moment. "That doesn't mean this situation is over, by any means. Whether Terra rises or falls, we have guaranteed that the Highlanders will continue on, exactly as they have in the past. They will change, they will adapt, and who knows, there may come a time when we are needed in a different role, in a different place..."

She looked up at him squarely. "If that time comes, I want the Highlanders to stay true to their covenants, to the history that brought them here. It would be one of the greatest honors of my life to know that the ideals of the Republic, the ideals cemented here, that were paid in blood, would continue on."

"You want something of the Republic to continue on, if the worst happens," Declan replied. "You want the Highlanders to carry on the traditions."

Her voice softened. "I am a child of two worlds, Dec. Surely you cannot blame me for wanting them to continue, even after I am gone."

He nodded slowly, and the two enjoyed a meaningful moment of silence.

"I could go back with you," Declan replied.

For a long moment, she seemed to consider it. The Twelfth Hastati Sentinels would be staying behind to garrison the planet until they received different orders, but he knew General McNamara would allow him to go with the Highlanders if he asked. The moment stretched on long enough for him to feel a little hope in his heart, but as she glanced behind her into the hospital room, he knew she would refuse.

She placed a hand on his cheek, looking deeply into his eyes as she spoke. "There would be nothing I would like better...but I think we both know your place is here."

Declan nodded, and she stepped back, turning as if to leave. She hesitated for a moment, however, and gave him an insouciant smile. "I suppose you could say that, with everything going on, there is no one else I would want to watch over my planet."

He was about to send a cutting response back, but instead he just smiled. Moving slowly, he reached to his own belt, drew her own knife, the knife she had given him in the Caithness Woods, and held it out to her with both hands as a gesture of respect.

Maeve took it from him reverently, and then sheathed it. For a long moment they just stood there, and then with a final, respectful nod, Lady Maeve Stirling turned and headed down the hallway, the soft *click* of her boots on the tile echoing down long after she was gone.

Declan slipped back into the room to find Bianca awake, her eyes focused on him. He smiled bravely and stepped over to her bedside. "Hey! I wasn't expecting you to be awake so soon."

"I've been in and out for a while. The doctors don't want me moving around too much. I'm a lot better off than some, but I got bounced around at the end there." Her expression turned serious, and she reached out to take his hand. "I heard about your grandfather, Dec. I am so sorry."

Something seemed to rip free in his chest, and it took all of his control to keep from breaking down. For several long moments he just gripped the rails of her bed tightly, his eyes clenched shut, the yawning chasm of pain in his chest like an open wound. For a long moment, all he could feel was the ache, until Bianca's hand slid over his own, the warmth keeping some of the cold chill within him at bay.

When he could finally speak, he barely recognized his own voice. "He died protecting those he loved, on the soil of the planet he fought and bled for. I wish he was still here...but I believe this is exactly the way he would want to go if he had the choice."

"He was an extraordinary man," she said, carefully pulling herself up to a sitting position.

This time, his vision started to blur. "That he was," Declan agreed, not trusting himself to say anything more.

Bianca carefully switched topics, giving him a moment to compose himself. "What happened after I was pulled out?"

"We redistributed our forces to cover the Capellans. With the Kuritans departing, we were able to move our artillery units to cover the spaceport, which was the final straw. The Capellans couldn't afford to lose their DropShips, so they decided on taking the wiser course of valor. I don't think they'll be back." He smiled thinly. "We also got to keep a healthy amount of salvage, which will help us build back up again."

She nodded, smiling at the news. The damage report on his *Marauder II* had been severe, but the countess had made it clear that he was to be near the top of the list for a replacement BattleMech if his could not be repaired.

"And the compound?" she asked. "The HPG?"

"It...took a lot of damage. The countess loaded two hover transports full of explosives, and..." Declan winced. "There's honestly not much of it left."

Bianca sat up a little straighter, but she didn't seem as distraught by the news as he'd expected. "It's probably not nearly as bad as it looks," she said. "Most of the critical items are underground for just such a reason. It probably looks terrible, and it might take time to rebuild it, but we should be able to get it up and running eventually."

Declan shook his head. "That's comforting to know, but it's still a major loss. The countess said it was a carefully calculated risk, that we needed to give the Kuritans a good reason to disengage. Without the HPG to fight over, there was little reason to stay. But it sounds like the countess banked on our enemies not knowing the vital parts of the HPG had survived the blast."

Something flashed in her eyes, and Declan squeezed her hand gently. "Regardless of what happened, the important thing is that you are safe."

She smiled weakly at him. "Is the countess leaving?"

"Yes," Declan replied, his own sadness slipping through at the thought. Tara Campbell had come to him personally after the battle to apologize for his grandfather's death, and he could see the raw edge of hurt in her own eyes as he relayed the final moments in the compound. Having to fight another battle on her beloved planet had seemed to age her further, and he remembered her dark, haunted look when she returned from a visit to her namesake city. "Her DropShips are ensuring that the Capellans and Kuritans leave the system, and then will be returning to Terra to support the defense there."

"And then what?" she asked. "The Capellans and Kuritans are gone, but not forever. The Republic is going to be fighting for its life on Terra, and the countess is gone... What do we do now?"

Declan sensed concern for herself in the question as well. She had seen ComStar brought to its knees in her lifetime, a situation many would never have thought possible, and now her role in Project Sunlight was over until they could get the HPG back up and running. If she was right about the HPG's vital components surviving, he imagined the research data she had come to Northwind for might still be recoverable, but the repair work on the HPG's dish and exterior structures would likely take years.

"Well, if we are going to get the HPG back up and running, we'll certainly need some HPG experts..." he said. "Also, the Highlanders that stayed here are going to have a busy time reorganizing, and we have a lot of damage to rebuild. We could use all the help we can get."

"We?" she noted, her eyes flashing in pleasure this time.

Declan shrugged, keeping the moment light, but when he spoke, the words were heavy with meaning. His free hand slipped to his waist, and the knife in the sheath at his side, sliding his thumb over the Casey family crest.

"Northwind takes care of its own."

CHAPTER 20

"It's a sair ficht for half a loaf."

—Scottish saying

UNKNOWN LOCATION
11 DECEMBER 3150

Maxwell Cheng worried at his straps for the hundredth time, attempting to get free from the bed where he was restrained. Whoever had strapped him down was a professional, and while the padded cuffs were not tearing into his wrists, he did not have enough slack to move a centimeter.

From the gentle thrum he could feel through the angled panel, he suspected he was on a DropShip under thrust. He must have been sedated for the transfer to the DropShip, probably done in a clandestine manner to avoid being seen by the Highlanders. While he was not sure if they would have fought to keep him on-planet, he was quite sure several Highlanders would have wanted a brief discussion with him before he was taken to Terra.

"I see believe you have an inkling of where we are," a voice said from behind him, and he watched a subdued shape move into his peripheral vision. He could not make out many details, but it appeared to be a man dressed in a gray Republic uniform, but he could not see any identifying information other than the Republic of the Sphere patch on his shoulder. From the careful posture and the careless way that this visitor wore the uniform, Cheng recognized him as another member of the interstellar brotherhood of intelligence operatives, someone as comfortable in this uniform as any other, and for whom rank was no longer a concern.

"I won't answer your questions," Cheng said. "I have been trained by the best in the Confederation, and we both know I would sooner die than give up any information."

The man smiled and shook his head, then reached into a small box that had been secured to a nearby table. "That can be arranged…"

He had just removed a wicked-looking knife from the box when a feminine voice from behind him spoke. "I will take it from here, Agent."

Cheng attempted to twist around to see his savior, but was forced to take solace in the disappointment on his interrogator's face. The Republic operative made a careful show of putting away his instrument and then departed from the room without another word.

The sound of footsteps drew Cheng's attention to his side as Lady Maeve Stirling stepped into view.

"I hope you don't think such a basic ploy is going to earn you my sympathies," Cheng said, pulling at his straps again. "I would hope you have a little more respect for my intelligence than that."

"I don't believe I have been seeing much intelligence of any kind, Mr. Cheng," Stirling replied, and she gestured to the two Republic guards who waited outside the door. One of them nodded, and the door closed with a *hiss*. "So I would not presume upon your value."

As soon as the doors had fully sealed, Cheng slumped forward in relief, giving her a withering glare. "Cutting it a little close there, don't you think? Another few moments and your man would have pulled out the hot pokers."

"Maybe you deserve it," Stirling replied playfully, moving to undo the bindings on his wrists. "Disappearing for nearly a week before making yourself known... Do you know how much time we wasted looking for you?"

"I was stuck behind enemy lines at the spaceport!" Cheng complained bitterly as she adjusted the table to a more convenient angle and unfastened the bracers at his ankles. "I didn't expect the entire Capellan force to seal me in!"

"Well, maybe you should've thought of that before blowing up one of their shuttles," she countered.

Cheng rubbed the feeling back into his wrists. "Thank you. They were starting to chafe. As for the spaceport, next time *you* come up with the exit plan. I just hope it was worth it. We just blew five years' worth of cover work with this little stunt." He stretched lithely, releasing a satisfied sigh as several joints cracked. "Paladin Lakewood is going to have a fit when she finds out."

"She knows that needs must better than anyone else I know," Stirling replied. "It had to be done, and there's no going back now. We had the opportunity to not only shatter the back of the Capellan strike on Northwind, but we also opened up a fault line between the Capellan Confederation and the Draconis Combine. It's not what we originally intended, but this battle might have just become one of the defining moments of the Republic."

"I just hope you remember that when Lakewood has us both in her office, explaining the term 'mission creep' in excruciating detail," Cheng replied glumly, getting an arch look from the Republic Knight. "My mission was to convince the Capellans to split their forces between the two continents, and I succeeded. I saw nothing in the mission brief about sabotaging a pact between two of the Great Houses all by myself."

"Needs must, Maxwell," Stirling replied. "You know as well as I that as soon as the Kuritans came to the party, all bets were off. I'm only glad we had you available to keep things from boiling over."

Stirling glanced out the viewport, getting a fleeting glimpse of Northwind, which twinkled as the DropShip burned farther away. Maxwell Cheng, loyal son of the Republic, had been a deep-cover operative for the Republic buried within the Maskirovka hierarchy. While his fellow Mask agents never fully trusted him—at least not enough to move him any closer to Sian than Northwind—his hawkish nature toward both the Combine and the Republic had served him in excellent stead, allowing him to be poised to act when the time was right.

Cheng had also been her ace in the hole in the Capellan hierarchy. By convincing the Grand Master that the Republic forces were hiding their greatest threat on Kearney, he had prodded them to split their forces, keeping them from striking the Twelfth Hastati with overwhelming force at the very outset of the invasion. If the Grand Master had combined his troops, moving against the limited Republic garrison on the planet, the Twelfth would never have survived long enough for the Grey Watch to reveal itself and come to the rescue.

Seeing his expression darken, she quickly changed the subject. "Bianca didn't balk at damaging the HPG?"

"Oh, she screamed bloody murder," Cheng replied, looking unusually sheepish. "She's old-school ComStar, so she never really shook her instinctive respect for HPG technology. Her family were some of Malcolm Buhl's Blessed Order loyalists. I think she only took the Project Sunlight gig to try redeeming herself in her own eyes."

"Well, she certainly did that," Stirling said. "Regardless, if we are to guarantee that the Draconis Combine pulls out of the Unity Pact, Ikeda needs to get back to the Combine before the Capellans can send their own message. At this rate, his explanation should get to the Coordinator before any message can reach the Chancellor, so I have no doubt the Unity Pact will no longer be a threat...at least to the Republic."

Cheng nodded, agreeing with at least that much of the Knight's thoughts. It had been a calculated risk, using the ComStar adept as a catspaw to convince Baxter to take the steps that had led to the final break between the two allies, but Bianca had performed wonderfully. Playing off the Fourth MAC commander's instinctive distrust for the Maskirovka, the two of them had ensured Baxter made the right jump when the time came.

"You never did tell me exactly how Bianca was injured," Stirling said suspiciously.

The sheepish look that he gave her was enough to make her laugh. "Well...we had to make it look *real*."

"You play a dangerous game, Mr. Cheng," Stirling replied playfully. "If Tucker Harwell finds out you damaged one of his savants, even Janella Lakewood won't be able to save you."

Cheng sat down on one of the acceleration couches on the inner bulkhead of the room. "We'll just have to make sure she never finds out then, won't we?"

"That depends on what you brought for the occasion."

Cheng smiled and gestured to the small box magnetically secured to the floor. Stirling opened the latches with a deft flick of her hands, and then whistled appreciatively. Reaching into the container, she pulled out the sealed travel decanter of Highlands Whisky and two zero-G bulbs. Tucking them under her arm, she also retrieved a small travel pouch of Glengarry cigars and placed it in the breast pocket of her jumpsuit. While they could get away with drinking at this point, they couldn't risk incurring the captain's wrath by lighting up in his precious DropShip. She handed the whisky to Cheng, who deftly poured them a pair of drinks and secured the bottle.

Cheng caught a glimpse of her eyes lingering on the box, and spoke without being asked. "A peace offering. Our remaining asset is continuing his mission... He sent these as a gift, to ensure there were no hard feelings."

Stirling took a deep breath, and then let it out, the only sign she had heard him at all.

"Do you think they're going to be all right?" Cheng asked as he handed her a bulb.

She took it gratefully, and then gazed back to the viewport as she sat in the other acceleration couch.

"I think they are going to fare better than we will." Stirling sipped and made a happy sound at the taste of her homeworld. "We're jumping back into the fire, and we both know one of the Clans will be at our doorstep sooner than later. We blunted the Capellan threat, but there is only so much we can do before we return to Terra."

"And what are you going to do when you get there?" Cheng asked before taking his own sip.

"I'm going home," Stirling replied, and he looked up at her in surprise. "My unit has been seconded to Campbell's Highlanders for the upcoming defense, and I intend to be at their side, no matter what happens. You?"

Cheng shrugged lightly. "The usual—mischief, mayhem, marauding. You never know where a Ghost Knight's life may lead."

"Well, then..." She lifted her whisky bulb. "Here's to whatever awaits us."

Cheng nodded, and lifted his whisky in return, and together the two watched the pearlescent orb of Northwind fade into the distance.

EPILOGUE

"It's a lang road that's no goat a turnin'."

—Scottish saying

PRIVATE OFFICE OF THE EXARCH
GENEVA, TERRA
REPUBLIC OF THE SPHERE
27 DECEMBER 3150

Not much had changed from when Countess Tara Campbell had last graced this office, at least on the surface. Although Maeve Stirling accompanied her this time, the weather was still foul, the room far too spartan, and the inhabitants far too grim. Still, she walked purposefully into the Exarch's inner sanctum, nodding to both Paladin Lakewood, the head of Republic intelligence, and Tucker Harwell, the Exarch's personal advisor and the head of Project Sunlight, before facing the Exarch himself.

"It seems you were successful in your efforts," Devlin Stone noted, his aged, gravelly voice holding a rare note of pleasure. "I can't say I am surprised, nor am I disappointed."

"We could only have done so thanks to your help, Exarch," Tara replied, inclining her head to the centenarian-plus leader of the Republic. "You kept your promise to Northwind, and that will be remembered. As I have promised, my forces are here to stand with you, no matter what may come."

"And they are welcome," Stone said. "When the Northwind Highlanders first chose to fly under the banner of the Republic, you became a vital part of breathing life into this mad dream. It is only fitting that you are here at the cusp of what we have built, as someone who will continue to uphold our traditions and goals as we move forward into a new age."

"Yet what of your allegiance?" the Exarch asked, a true note of curiosity in his voice. "You have sworn an oath to the Republic, yet you speak of your own forces, who fight under the banner of the Northwind Highlanders. Do you not feel a conflict of interest there?"

"No, Exarch," Tara replied simply. "I was born a Highlander, and a Highlander I shall always be. Yet I swore myself to a covenant with the Republic, like my mother and father before me. At this point in history, to be a Highlander is to be one with the Republic, and I am honored to fight beside my kin in its defense."

The Exarch nodded, and his eyes moved to Maeve. "I suppose you're of the same mind as the countess, my lady?"

"Only to a point, Exarch," Maeve replied. "While we have both sworn ourselves to the service to the Republic, my oath as a Knight of the Republic is slightly different than hers. I will fight with my unit, and I will give my all to the cause of the Republic, as I always have."

Stone nodded, and for a moment Tara thought she saw a glimmer of sadness in his eyes. Was this what he had expected, so long ago? Did he think this was the way that things were going to be?

The Exarch turned back to Tara. "And what of the Grey Watch?"

"Their numbers were sorely depleted in the fighting. They would all have come with us if I had asked, but between their mandate to protect Northwind and the condition of the official garrison, I thought it best that they stay to rest and rearm. Colonel Griffin did bring one of his battalions with us, however, so the Grey Watch will be here to uphold their part of our covenant."

The Exarch nodded. Tara had delivered her response with the holo-drama perfection expected of her, but it was too polished of an answer, something she wanted to believe was true.

Still, whatever the choice would be, she was sure the Highlanders would do what they had always done. The choices had been theirs, as always, and they had taken it.

Tara recalled a conversation with Maeve on the bridge of her DropShip during their journey from Northwind. "What was different this time?" Maeve had asked, and Tara had smiled at her before focusing back on the starscape.

"Each time that others came to us and asked us for something," she had explained, "we traditionally found ourselves on the short end of the stick, fighting for those who would give us nary a second thought. Stone...he's a wily ol' so-and-so, but he never did us wrong. Especially now... When Northwind needed him, Republic forces answered the call first, and he sent Republic reinforcements when they were needed, despite him sorely needing them on Terra as well. He made the choice to uphold the covenant he had made with us, without asking for anything in return. That's what made him different...and that is why we will follow him into battle."

Tara smiled slightly at the memory, although she endeavored to keep her expression neutral as the Exarch finished updating her on everything that had happened during her absence. Then he gave her instructions to head to the redoubt that had been prepared for the Highlanders in France.

Expecting to be dismissed, she was surprised when the Exarch sent Lakewood and Harwell away instead. Paladin Lakewood gave her a small smile before departing, and then the two Highlanders were left alone with the Exarch of the Republic.

Stone stepped around the desk, moving toward the bay window that looked out over Geneva, and stared out thoughtfully for several moments before speaking. "Countess, I would like your help with something, if you could."

"Anything, Exarch," Tara replied without hesitation. "I serve the Republic."

A grim smile painted Stone's features. "You might not want to be so quick to agree until you have learned what I have in mind," he said. "I want you to agree to a new covenant."

Tara straightened in surprise. "Another covenant, Exarch? We are still bound to our duty to the Republic..."

Stone shook his head. "We both know that while the Capellans may no longer be a threat to Terra, that they were never the greatest threat."

Tara nodded, knowing the dark truth that plagued the Exarch's cunning mind was rearing its ugly head once again. Both Clan Wolf and Clan Jade Falcon were poised to strike at Terra, and they would stop at nothing to achieve their goal of conquest. While the Capellans had been knocked back on their heels, an attack from either Clan would be a far more deadly proposition, for they had leveraged their entire way of life on successfully claiming the birthworld of humanity.

The Exarch's eyes locked on the view outside his window, but he seemed to be thousands of kilometers away. "While I have every faith that we will stop the invaders cold when they finally come, young Mr. Harwell has reminded me that it is the greatest of hubris to believe no one will ever topple the Republic from our place on Terra. I'm sure that House Cameron felt the same way during the time of the Terran Hegemony and the first Star League, and the last thing I would want is to be remembered the same way.

"As such," he continued, taking the two Highlanders back under his gaze, "I want you to make me a new covenant: if the worst should happen, if the Republic should fall the way of the Star League and the Terran Hegemony...I want something of our ideals to endure. I want you to carry on the traditions, as you always have. The Black Watch, the Grey Watch—the Highlanders themselves have always carried on the traditions they hold so dearly. If the worst should happen...I want to know that we will be remembered."

For a long moment, there was nothing but silence in the cavernous office, a solemn conversation neither she nor the Exarch needed to speak aloud. After several long, meaningful moments, Tara nodded, and Stone returned the gesture before turning back to look over Geneva, and the world he had vowed to protect.

Tara turned to Maeve and nodded. Both women stiffened to attention for a moment, then returned to the double doors at the end of the room, careful to maintain the silence until they reached the hallway.

But before the doors closed behind them, Tara stole one last glance at the aging Exarch, trying to forever burn into her memory the way he stood, stoically, focusing on how all of this could eventually end.

She would not forget that sight as long as she lived.

ABOUT THE AUTHOR

Michael J. Ciaravella has been a passionate devotee of the *BattleTech* universe for over twenty years, most recently having the honor of writing the "Secrets of the Sphere" articles for the new *BattleTech* Magazine, *Shrapnel*. A regular sight on the convention circuit, Michael has earned multiple championship titles, including several *BattleTech* Open and Solaris Melee Championships as well as the coveted Pryde Bloodname. In what little free time he has not devoted to writing and gaming pursuits, Michael is also an award-winning theatrical producer, director, and actor in New York, where he lives with his beloved Amy and their three cats: Tuxberious Nova Cat, Pancetta Kurita, and Princess Waffles Francesca Peregrine.

BATTLETECH GLOSSARY

AUTOCANNON

A rapid-fire, auto-loading weapon. Light autocannons range from 30 to 90 millimeter (mm), and heavy autocannons may be from 80 to 120mm or more. They fire high-speed streams of high-explosive, armor-piercing shells.

BATTLEMECH

BattleMechs are the most powerful war machines ever built. First developed by Terran scientists and engineers, these huge vehicles are faster, more mobile, better-armored and more heavily armed than any twentieth-century tank. Ten to twelve meters tall and equipped with particle projection cannons, lasers, rapid-fire autocannon and missiles, they pack enough firepower to flatten anything but another BattleMech. A small fusion reactor provides virtually unlimited power, and BattleMechs can be adapted to fight in environments ranging from sun-baked deserts to subzero arctic icefields.

DROPSHIPS

Because interstellar JumpShips must avoid entering the heart of a solar system, they must "dock" in space at a considerable distance from a system's inhabited worlds. DropShips were developed for interplanetary travel. As the name implies, a DropShip is attached to hardpoints on the JumpShip's drive core, later to be dropped from the parent vessel after in-system entry. Though incapable of FTL travel, DropShips are highly maneuverable, well-armed and sufficiently aerodynamic to take off from and land on a planetary surface. The journey from the jump point to the inhabited worlds of a system usually requires a normal-space journey of several days or weeks, depending on the type of star.

FLAMER

Flamethrowers are a small but time-honored anti-infantry weapon in vehicular arsenals. Whether fusion-based or fuel-based, flamers spew fire in a tight beam that "splashes" against a target, igniting almost anything it touches.

GAUSS RIFLE

This weapon uses magnetic coils to accelerate a solid nickel-ferrous slug about the size of a football at an enemy target, inflicting massive damage through sheer kinetic impact at long range and with little heat. However, the accelerator coils and the slug's supersonic speed mean that while the Gauss rifle is smokeless and lacks the flash of an autocannon, it has a much more potent report that can shatter glass.

INDUSTRIALMECH

Also known as WorkMechs or UtilityMechs, they are large, bipedal or quadrupedal machines used for industrial purposes (hence the name). They are similar in shape to BattleMechs, which they predate, and feature many of the same technologies, but are built for non-combat tasks such as construction, farming, and policing.

JUMPSHIPS

Interstellar travel is accomplished via JumpShips, first developed in the twenty-second century. These somewhat ungainly vessels consist of a long, thin drive core and a sail resembling an enormous parasol, which can extend up to a kilometer in width. The ship is named for its ability to "jump" instantaneously across vast distances of space. After making its jump, the ship cannot travel until it has recharged by gathering up more solar energy.

The JumpShip's enormous sail is constructed from a special metal that absorbs vast quantities of electromagnetic energy from the nearest star. When it has soaked up enough energy, the sail transfers it to the drive core, which converts it into a space-twisting field. An instant later, the ship arrives at the next jump point, a distance of up to thirty light-years. This field is known as hyperspace, and its discovery opened to mankind the gateway to the stars.

JumpShips never land on planets. Interplanetary travel is carried out by DropShips, vessels that are attached to the JumpShip until arrival at the jump point.

LASER

An acronym for "Light Amplification through Stimulated Emission of Radiation." When used as a weapon, the laser damages the target by concentrating extreme heat onto a small area. BattleMech lasers are designated as small, medium or large. Lasers are also available as shoulder-fired weapons operating from a portable backpack power unit. Certain range-finders and targeting equipment also employ low-level lasers.

LRM

Abbreviation for "Long-Range Missile," an indirect-fire missile with a high-explosive warhead.

MACHINE GUN

A small autocannon intended for anti-personnel assaults. Typically non-armor-penetrating, machine guns are often best used against infantry, as they can spray a large area with relatively inexpensive fire.

PARTICLE PROJECTION CANNON (PPC)

One of the most powerful and long-range energy weapons on the battlefield, a PPC fires a stream of charged particles that outwardly functions as a bright blue laser, but also throws off enough static discharge to resemble a bolt of manmade lightning. The kinetic and heat impact of a PPC is enough to cause the vaporization of armor and structure alike, and most PPCs have the power to kill a pilot in his machine through an armor-penetrating headshot.

SRM

The abbreviation for "Short-Range Missile," a direct-trajectory missile with high-explosive or armor-piercing explosive warheads. They have a range of less than one kilometer and are only reliably accurate at ranges of less than 300 meters. They are more powerful, however, than LRMs.

SUCCESSOR LORDS

After the fall of the first Star League, the remaining members of the High Council each asserted his or her right to become First Lord. Their star empires became known as the Successor States and the rulers as Successor Lords. The Clan Invasion temporarily interrupted centuries of warfare known as the Succession Wars, which first began in 2786.

BATTLETECH ERAS

The *BattleTech* universe is a living, vibrant entity that grows each year as more sourcebooks and fiction are published. A dynamic universe, its setting and characters evolve over time within a highly detailed continuity framework, bringing everything to life in a way a static game universe cannot match.

To help quickly and easily convey the timeline of the universe—and to allow a player to easily "plug in" a given novel or sourcebook—we've divided *BattleTech* into six major eras.

STAR LEAGUE
(Present–2780)

Ian Cameron, ruler of the Terran Hegemony, concludes decades of tireless effort with the creation of the Star League, a political and military alliance between all Great Houses and the Hegemony. Star League armed forces immediately launch the Reunification War, forcing the Periphery realms to join. For the next two centuries, humanity experiences a golden age across the thousand light-years of human-occupied space known as the Inner Sphere. It also sees the creation of the most powerful military in human history.

(This era also covers the centuries before the founding of the Star League in 2571, most notably the Age of War.)

SUCCESSION WARS
(2781–3049)

Every last member of First Lord Richard Cameron's family is killed during a coup launched by Stefan Amaris. Following the thirteen-year war to unseat him, the rulers of each of the five Great Houses disband the Star League. General Aleksandr Kerensky departs with eighty percent of the Star League Defense Force beyond known space and the Inner Sphere collapses into centuries of warfare known as the Succession Wars that will eventually result in a massive loss of technology across most worlds.

CLAN INVASION
(3050–3061)

A mysterious invading force strikes the coreward region of the Inner Sphere. The invaders, called the Clans, are descendants of Kerensky's SLDF troops, forged into a society dedicated to becoming the greatest fighting force in history. With vastly superior technology and warriors, the Clans conquer world after world. Eventually this outside threat will forge a new Star League, something hundreds of years of warfare failed to accomplish. In addition, the Clans will act as a catalyst for a technological renaissance.

CIVIL WAR
(3062–3067)

The Clan threat is eventually lessened with the complete destruction of a Clan. With that massive external threat apparently neutralized, internal conflicts explode around the Inner Sphere. House Liao conquers its former Commonality, the St. Ives Compact; a rebellion of military units belonging to House Kurita sparks a war with their powerful border enemy, Clan Ghost Bear; the fabulously powerful Federated Commonwealth of House Steiner and House Davion collapses into five long years of bitter civil war.

JIHAD
(3067–3080)

Following the Federated Commonwealth Civil War, the leaders of the Great Houses meet and disband the new Star League, declaring it a sham. The pseudo-religious Word of Blake—a splinter group of ComStar, the protectors and controllers of interstellar communication—launch the Jihad: an interstellar war that pits every faction against each other and even against themselves, as weapons of mass destruction are used for the first time in centuries while new and frightening technologies are also unleashed.

DARK AGE
(3081-3150)

Under the guidance of Devlin Stone, the Republic of the Sphere is born at the heart of the Inner Sphere following the Jihad. One of the more extensive periods of peace begins to break out as the 32nd century dawns. The factions, to one degree or another, embrace disarmament, and the massive armies of the Succession Wars begin to fade. However, in 3132 eighty percent of interstellar communications collapses, throwing the universe into chaos. Wars erupt almost immediately, and the factions begin rebuilding their armies.

ILCLAN
(3151-present)

The once-invulnerable Republic of the Sphere lies in ruins, torn apart by the Great Houses and the Clans as they wage war against each other on a scale not seen in nearly a century. Mercenaries flourish once more, selling their might to the highest bidder. As Fortress Republic collapses, the Clans race toward Terra to claim their long-denied birthright and create a supreme authority that will fulfill the dream of Aleksandr Kerensky and rule the Inner Sphere by any means necessary: The ilClan.

LOOKING FOR MORE HARD HITTING BATTLETECH FICTION?

WE'LL GET YOU RIGHT BACK INTO THE BATTLE!

Catalyst Game Labs brings you the very best in *BattleTech* fiction, available at most ebook retailers, including Amazon, Apple Books, Kobo, Barnes & Noble, and more!

NOVELS

1. *Decision at Thunder Rift* by William H. Keith Jr.
2. *Mercenary's Star* by William H. Keith Jr.
3. *The Price of Glory* by William H. Keith, Jr.
4. *Warrior: En Garde* by Michael A. Stackpole
5. *Warrior: Riposte* by Michael A. Stackpole
6. *Warrior: Coupé* by Michael A. Stackpole
7. Wolves on the Border by Robert N. Charrette
8. *Heir to the Dragon* by Robert N. Charrette
9. *Lethal Heritage* (The Blood of Kerensky, Volume 1) by Michael A. Stackpole
10. *Blood Legacy* (The Blood of Kerensky, Volume 2) by Michael A. Stackpole
11. *Lost Destiny* (The Blood of Kerensky, Volume 3) by Michael A. Stackpole
12. *Way of the Clans* (Legend of the Jade Phoenix, Volume 1) by Robert Thurston
13. *Bloodname* (Legend of the Jade Phoenix, Volume 2) by Robert Thurston
14. *Falcon Guard* (Legend of the Jade Phoenix, Volume 3) by Robert Thurston
15. *Wolf Pack* by Robert N. Charrette
16. *Main Event* by James D. Long
17. *Natural Selection* by Michael A. Stackpole
18. *Assumption of Risk* by Michael A. Stackpole
19. *Blood of Heroes* by Andrew Keith
20. *Close Quarters* by Victor Milán
21. *Far Country* by Peter L. Rice
22. *D.R.T.* by James D. Long
23. *Tactics of Duty* by William H. Keith
24. *Bred for War* by Michael A. Stackpole
25. *I Am Jade Falcon* by Robert Thurston
26. *Highlander Gambit* by Blaine Lee Pardoe
27. *Hearts of Chaos* by Victor Milán
28. *Operation Excalibur* by William H. Keith
29. *Malicious Intent* by Michael A. Stackpole
30. *Black Dragon* by Victor Milán
31. *Impetus of War* by Blaine Lee Pardoe
32. *Double-Blind* by Loren L. Coleman
33. *Binding Force* by Loren L. Coleman
34. *Exodus Road* (Twilight of the Clans, Volume 1) by Blaine Lee Pardoe
35. *Grave Covenant* ((Twilight of the Clans, Volume 2) by Michael A. Stackpole

36. *The Hunters* (Twilight of the Clans, Volume 3) by Thomas S. Gressman
37. *Freebirth* (Twilight of the Clans, Volume 4) by Robert Thurston
38. *Sword and Fire* (Twilight of the Clans, Volume 5) by Thomas S. Gressman
39. *Shadows of War* (Twilight of the Clans, Volume 6) by Thomas S. Gressman
40. *Prince of Havoc* (Twilight of the Clans, Volume 7) by Michael A. Stackpole
41. *Falcon Rising* (Twilight of the Clans, Volume 8) by Robert Thurston
42. *Threads of Ambition* (The Capellan Solution, Book 1) by Loren L. Coleman
43. *The Killing Fields* (The Capellan Solution, Book 2) by Loren L. Coleman
44. *Dagger Point* by Thomas S. Gressman
45. *Ghost of Winter* by Stephen Kenson
46. *Roar of Honor* by Blaine Lee Pardoe
47. *By Blood Betrayed* by Blaine Lee Pardoe and Mel Odom
48. *Illusions of Victory* by Loren L. Coleman
49. *Flashpoint* by Loren L. Coleman
50. *Measure of a Hero* by Blaine Lee Pardoe
51. *Path of Glory* by Randall N. Bills
52. *Test of Vengeance* by Bryan Nystul
53. *Patriots and Tyrants* by Loren L. Coleman
54. *Call of Duty* by Blaine Lee Pardoe
55. *Initiation to War* by Robert N. Charrette
56. *The Dying Time* by Thomas S. Gressman
57. *Storms of Fate* by Loren L. Coleman
58. *Imminent Crisis* by Randall N. Bills
59. *Operation Audacity* by Blaine Lee Pardoe
60. *Endgame* by Loren L. Coleman
61. *A Bonfire of Worlds* by Steven Mohan, Jr.
62. *Ghost War* by Michael A. Stackpole
63. *A Call to Arms* by Loren L. Coleman
64. *Isle of the Blessed* by Steven Mohan, Jr.
65. *Embers of War* by Jason Schmetzer
66. *Betrayal of Ideals* by Blaine Lee Pardoe
67. *Forever Faithful* by Blaine Lee Pardoe
68. *Kell Hounds Ascendant* by Michael A. Stackpole
69. *Redemption Rift* by Jason Schmetzer
70. *Grey Watch Protocol* (The Highlander Covenant, Book One) by Michael J. Ciaravella
71. *Honor's Gauntlet* by Bryan Young
72. *Icons of War* by Craig A. Reed, Jr.
73. *Children of Kerensky* by Blaine Lee Pardoe
74. *Hour of the Wolf* by Blaine Lee Pardoe
75. *Fall From Glory* (Founding of the Clans, Book One) by Randall N. Bills
76. *Paid in Blood* (The Highlander Covenant, Book Two) by Michael J. Ciaravella

YOUNG ADULT NOVELS

1. *The Nellus Academy Incident* by Jennifer Brozek
2. *Iron Dawn* (Rogue Academy, Book 1) by Jennifer Brozek
3. *Ghost Hour* (Rogue Academy, Book 2) by Jennifer Brozek

OMNIBUSES

1. *The Gray Death Legion Trilogy* by William H. Keith, Jr.

NOVELLAS/SHORT STORIES

1. *Lion's Roar* by Steven Mohan, Jr.
2. *Sniper* by Jason Schmetzer
3. *Eclipse* by Jason Schmetzer
4. *Hector* by Jason Schmetzer
5. *The Frost Advances (Operation Ice Storm, Part 1)* by Jason Schmetzer
6. *The Winds of Spring (Operation Ice Storm, Part 2)* by Jason Schmetzer
7. *Instrument of Destruction (Ghost Bear's Lament, Part 1)* by Steven Mohan, Jr.
8. *The Fading Call of Glory (Ghost Bear's Lament, Part 2)* by Steven Mohan, Jr.
9. *Vengeance* by Jason Schmetzer
10. *A Splinter of Hope* by Philip A. Lee
11. *The Anvil* by Blaine Lee Pardoe
12. *A Splinter of Hope/The Anvil* (omnibus)
13. *Not the Way the Smart Money Bets (Kell Hounds Ascendant #1)* by Michael A. Stackpole
14. *A Tiny Spot of Rebellion (Kell Hounds Ascendant #2)* by Michael A. Stackpole
15. *A Clever Bit of Fiction (Kell Hounds Ascendant #3)* by Michael A. Stackpole
16. *Break-Away (Proliferation Cycle #1)* by Ilsa J. Bick
17. *Prometheus Unbound (Proliferation Cycle #2)* by Herbert A. Beas II
18. *Nothing Ventured (Proliferation Cycle #3)* by Christoffer Trossen
19. *Fall Down Seven Times, Get Up Eight (Proliferation Cycle #4)* by Randall N. Bills
20. *A Dish Served Cold (Proliferation Cycle #5)* by Chris Hartford and Jason M. Hardy
21. *The Spider Dances (Proliferation Cycle #6)* by Jason Schmetzer
22. *Shell Games* by Jason Schmetzer
23. *Divided We Fall* by Blaine Lee Pardoe
24. *The Hunt for Jardine (Forgotten Worlds, Part One)* by Herbert A. Beas II
25. *Rock of the Republic* by Blaine Lee Pardoe
26. *Finding Jardine (Forgotten Worlds, Part Two)* by Herbert A. Beas II

ANTHOLOGIES

1. *The Corps (BattleCorps Anthology, Volume 1)* edited by Loren. L. Coleman
2. *First Strike (BattleCorps Anthology, Volume 2)* edited by Loren L. Coleman
3. *Weapons Free (BattleCorps Anthology, Volume 3)* edited by Jason Schmetzer
4. *Onslaught: Tales from the Clan Invasion* edited by Jason Schmetzer
5. *Edge of the Storm* by Jason Schmetzer
6. *Fire for Effect (BattleCorps Anthology, Volume 4)* edited by Jason Schmetzer
7. *Chaos Born (Chaos Irregulars, Book 1)* by Kevin Killiany
8. *Chaos Formed (Chaos Irregulars, Book 2)* by Kevin Killiany
9. *Counterattack (BattleCorps Anthology, Volume 5)* edited by Jason Schmetzer
10. *Front Lines (BattleCorps Anthology Volume 6)* edited by Jason Schmetzer and Philip A. Lee
11. *Legacy* edited by John Helfers and Philip A. Lee
12. *Kill Zone (BattleCorps Anthology Volume 7)* edited by Philip A. Lee
13. *Gray Markets (A BattleCorps Anthology),* edited by Jason Schmetzer and Philip A. Lee
14. *Slack Tide (A BattleCorps Anthology),* edited by Jason Schmetzer and Philip A. Lee
15. *The Battle of Tukayyid* edited by John Helfers

MAGAZINES

1. *Shrapnel* Issues #1–4

Made in the USA
Middletown, DE
23 November 2022

15564450R00080